From the ASHES

Athena Barnim

MORE BOOKS BY ATHENA BARNIM

Balsam River Series

One Life to Live

From the Ashes

Book 3 (Noah)- Coming late 2024

Cover Design: Ivan Semonchuk-MIBLART

Editor: Sarah Ward @sarahwardbooks

ASIN: E-book- B0CW1HZBV2

ISBN: Paperback- 9798880449064

ISBN: Hardback- 9798880449156

FOR BEC, ALWAYS.

And for Jordon, Aaron, Melanie & Eden

Because the weight of grief is lighter when you carry it with me.

CONTENT WARNING

This story involves many sensitive topics including but not limited to, grief and loss, loss of sibling (off page, in the past), loss of parent (off page, in the past) and trauma/grief due to fire.

My hope is that I have written about these in a way that is sensitive to readers but also in such a manner that raises awareness for those that don't have personal experience with these topics.

Please take care of your mental health and make the best choice for yourself whether to continue reading or not.

Much love to you all.

Contents

PROLOGUE

Four Years Earlier

Sara

I stand in the front pew as Jack squeezes my hand tightly. He must have felt me tense as the doors in the back opened.

"Oh fuck," I mutter, probably louder than I meant to. "I can't do this." He squeezes harder as the sobs wrack my body.

"You can, Sara, I've got you." Jack's gravelly voice breaks through the fog that is my mind. I can tell he's struggling to keep it together too.

They're walking my sister's casket down the aisle. My two brothers and my brother-in-law, Mark, are walking my sister's casket down the aisle. This is so fucked. Stoic, broken, and lost, all holding a handle as they perform this ridiculous task that no one should ever have to do.

How did we get here? When did this become who we are? People who've lost their sister, their wife, their daughter. I look over at my parents. Mom is hunched into herself; Dad's arm is around her shoulders. He's trying to stand tall as tears run down his face. We are all just a broken semblance of what we were just a week ago.

I don't know where we go from here. I don't know if I can make it through this hour, let alone the rest of my life without her. My gaze falls down to baby Andria. She's snuggled in a wrap in Jack's arms, oblivious to the loss that's surrounding her. She'll never know her sweet mama. How can I make sure she gets to know the very best parts of my beautiful sister?

I will, somehow. She will know that she had the very best mom. She'll know how much Amy loved her, even though she never got to meet her. But I can't think about that right now. All I can think about is the box slowly passing me that holds what's left of my very best friend. So many memories, so much life, stolen away in a second. Death and pain and sadness is what is in that box.

As they reach the front of the chapel, I push past Jack and rush into the aisle to my brothers' sides. I grab Liam and Noah and wrap an arm around each of their necks, holding them as tightly as I can. I open an arm for Mark to join us, but he stands just out of my grasp. It's not the first time this week I've felt like I can't reach him. Our combined sobs fill the chapel, and I don't want to step away from my brothers. Letting go of them at this moment feels like letting her go, and I can't do that.

It's just us, and Jack sitting with little Andria held tightly against his chest. He sits beside Mark's mom, and his sister, Jenna. Mark reaches his seat between them and takes his two-week-old daughter into his own arms. He rests his lips against the top of her head as tears stream down his cheeks. There's no one else here to see us fall apart, and it wouldn't even matter if they did.

Brokenness is all I see. Grief is drowning us all and we can't even save each other.

After the service everyone heads to my parents' farm. We'll all meet up there eventually for food and drinks and whatever else we're supposed to be doing, but right now I need to be alone. Throughout this past week I haven't been able to say what I need. I want to be with everyone that's as shattered as I am, but I also want to curl up in my bed by myself and never speak to anyone again. Finally, I know I need time alone.

I'm not stupid enough to think it will help.

I don't know if I will ever figure out how I'm going to go on with my life without Amy. I don't know how to be this person that doesn't have a sister. I'm supposed to have a sister.

My phone vibrates in my pocket, stopping the spiral that my brain was about to go on. I can't imagine who would have the nerve to text me today.

Jack: *We're all at the house, I'm going to assume you're out behind her place taking a minute alone, but just know I'm here if you need someone... someone that isn't the whole family all at once.*

I don't know how he always knows where I am and what I'm doing, but he's more in tune with me than half of the people over there. Maybe I let him in more than them because he doesn't expect anything from me. He doesn't judge how I'm a little different from the rest of them. I moved off the farm and like my own space; to be creative and to just be alone. And he seems to get it. He's been here for me this week more than anyone and I'm grateful to him for that. I shoot him back a quick reply, so he doesn't worry.

Sara: *Thanks J. I'll be there soon.*

I don't know how to thank him properly, so that will have to do for now.

I should head back. It's quite a long walk from my spot behind Amy and Mark's place to get back up to the main house and I don't even know how long I've been out here. They lived in a beautiful ranch-style house on the eastern edge of the family farm. She loved being so close to Mom and Dad, and they loved knowing they'd be close as their family grew and they raised their kids here.

Nothing will ever be the same for any of us. And it breaks my fucking heart.

We loved sitting back here in the quiet. The river our town is named after runs about two hundred feet away. The sound of it makes you feel like you're sitting in the wilderness when really, it's just Amy's backyard. This was our favourite spot to play as young girls, so she didn't think twice about where to build the home that she and Mark had planned since before they were married last year. The perfect place to raise Andi, and more kids one day, she'd hoped.

I'm about to make my way back to the main house when I hear a car door slam. As I come around the front corner of the house, I see it's not a car, but a truck. Mark's GMC to be exact. He has the truck bed full of bags and boxes and the back seat is crammed with more, tucked in around Andria sleeping in her car seat.

What the fuck is going on?

He interrupts that thought when he comes out the front door with a single suitcase in his hand. He stops in his tracks when he sees me.

"Shit." He curses as he sets the suitcase down and runs a hand over his short hair. He got it trimmed before Andria was born, before everything changed. Amy wanted him to look nice in pictures at the hospital. There were no pictures. Nothing went as they planned.

He looks anything but nice now, his eyes have a permanent red rim around them and black bags beneath. He looks like he hasn't shaved since that awful day; an unkept beard covers his jaw and cheeks. I want to wrap him in a hug but any time I come near him he stiffens like I might detonate an invisible bomb.

I look into his eyes now, and I know. He's leaving. They bounce from me and back to the truck where Andria is waiting for him.

"You're leaving, aren't you?"

Now he can't even look at me. Good. Fuck him. How can he do this? Was he even going to say goodbye? Where is he going? What is he thinking?

As if he can read all those thoughts in my mind, he rubs his face with his hands and says, "Sara, I'm sorry. I'm so sorry." His voice breaks as a sob escapes his throat and I can't help but go to him. I wrap my arms around him. He doesn't stiffen this time; he folds into me like I am all that's holding him upright.

"Mark, please. Please don't go," I beg him. "I know it's hard. But we can do it together. I don't know how but I know we can."

He pulls away quickly, wipes his eyes with the back of his hand while saying, "No. No, Sara, you don't know. I can't do anything that I need to, not here. I have to get away from this place. I'll call when I get where I'm going. Tell everyone that I'm sorry."

That's it. That's all he says, then walks to his truck, throws the suitcase in the passenger seat as he slides behind the wheel, and backs out of their driveway. His driveway. Amy's driveway. Now, nobody's driveway.

When I finally make my way back up to the house, Mom and Dad are sitting having coffee in the kitchen while everyone else is milling about aimlessly, eating, drinking, or just staring into space. Mrs. Davis and Jenna aren't here. Did they even come back? Do they know Mark is leaving town? I can't even wrap my head around how I'm supposed to tell everyone that he's gone. He took our little girl and left.

No, she's his little girl. She feels like ours because she is all we have left of Amy. He is her father and has every right to make decisions on her behalf. I just don't know if my family will see it that way.

I find Jack quickly, or he finds me. I'm never really too sure.

"Hey," he whispers from just behind me.

I turn to face him. "Thanks for checking in. I was just sitting in our spot. I just needed a minute."

"I know. None of this is easy. Jesus, Sara, I'm reeling here. I can't imagine what's going on in your head and your heart." He reaches out for me, and I step into his arms easily.

"Feels like I'm shattered. Just everything's broken; my heart, my soul, everything. I don't know what to do next. Jack, I don't know how to do life without her." The tears just won't stop. Every time I think there can't possibly be more, they start again. "Especially hard shit like this! Jack, I need her by my side to get through this. We had a deal. Always there for each other to lean on when shit got hard." I don't even know if he can understand me at this point, but I can't stop. "Why did she have to leave me here? Why her? Why not me instead?"

Jack snaps back from the embrace he's holding me in, his voice fierce, "Hey! I don't want to hear you say that shit again! Sara, I know this hurts and I know it doesn't make any fucking sense, but you will never wish it was you instead, ever!"

I don't know if I've ever heard Jack sound so angry with me. He's always been so soft and gentle, but apparently he's not done with the fierce protector role because he continues, "We will always wish it wasn't her, but I can't stand the thought of you wishing it was you. Sara, you have to see how crazy that is. Tell me you're hearing me!"

"I do. I know. I didn't mean it like that, not like I want to die, not really. I just don't know how to feel. I can't help but think of Andria and how much she needs her mother. She doesn't need me, not if Amy was here. I don't know... I just don't know anything anymore. I need to wake up and find out that this was all just a horrible dream."

Nightmare. I am living a nightmare, and I know in my soul that I am not going to wake up.

"Sometimes it's easy to remember her, and to tell stories and laugh together, but most of the time I can't wrap my mind around a memory because there will never be new ones. How can that be? How is this all we got? And Andria didn't get any of it! How can any of this be true? She's truly gone, and now Mark and Andria are gone too!" The last part comes out more as a wail and I can't stop the sobbing once it starts.

Jack pulls me away from his chest again, this time in shock. "Wait. What? Mark and the baby are gone? Gone where?"

I try to stop crying long enough to tell him what happened back at the house. I don't know how, but he gets the gist. He pulls me in and holds me tighter. I can't have what I truly need right now. I need my sister, but this is a close second. Thank God for good friends.

Jack

I don't know why I can't leave Sara Ryan alone. She's Noah's sister. Noah's awesome, though, so that's not really scaring me. These feelings I have for his sister are what's scaring me.

Noah and I have been friends for a long time but we weren't really close until after high school. We were a few of the only guys to stay in town after graduation. While everyone else chased the next big dream we decided to live the small town dream that meant staying in Balsam River. I took over my dad's Christmas tree farm almost right away and Noah went to college and got hired on the Balsam River Fire Department.

I didn't have a huge friend group before but those few years after everyone took off could've been dark if it wasn't for Noah and his upbeat, always happy personality. He pulls me out of my shell, and I'm not too dense to know that I need that. His younger brother, Liam, comes out to the farm with him sometimes and the three of us hike or play basketball. Sometimes we just sit and have a beer and chat about the town and our families. It might seem boring to some people, but it's everything to me. I can't do the city life, the corporate job, or nights out at bars with Noah, looking for women. I just want this; my farm, my town, and my friends.

Losing Amy has shaken the town, but I can't even begin to imagine the brokenness that the Ryan family is feeling. Noah tries to hide it well. He smiles enough and laughs a lot. He goes out to his favourite bars every weekend, but is that coping? Liam is acting more like me every day, secluded either at the farm or in his office at his coffee shop bookstore. Then there's Sara. Why can't I wrap my head around Sara?

I'd call myself a friend to anyone in this town who needs one. They've all watched me grow up and lent a hand when I needed them, to turn the farm around after dad let it go into disrepair. So, yeah, I'd definitely step up to help anyone else in need, but this is different. Sara is broken and I want to put her back together.

The thought of her grieving, struggling and drowning by herself, is enough to send me over the edge of insanity. Noah keeps telling me she's fine, but I can tell that Liam is worried and doesn't know what to do. It was always Sara and Amy, so she doesn't really have any girlfriends. Amy was her everything. Jenna Davis was close with them when they were younger, but they grew up without her and then just drifted apart. Mark skipping town with Andria would prevent that relationship from blooming again. Last I heard, Jenna was planning to head to Toronto for university in a few weeks too, so Sara truly has no one.

Fuck, why do I need to be her someone? My heart breaks a little more every time I look into her empty eyes, that's why. When I close mine, all I see is her. It's never been like this before. Is it grief? Guilt? I don't have anything to feel guilty for, but what is it called when you're grieving on behalf of someone else? I loved Amy as much as the next person. She was just one of those people, it was impossible not to love her. But it's seeing Sara hurting that's killing me. I see Noah and Liam going through the same thing, and their parents too, but it feels like more for Sara. It's like a tickle on the edge of my brain, my heart trying to tell me something that I'm not ready to understand. I am a fixer by nature, so maybe I just see a problem and need to be the solution.

She just needs a friend, I can be that, like I've always been. I told her I would show up, and regardless of how confused I am about these feelings, I will do that. Nothing can stop me.

CHAPTER

One

Sara

"Argh!" I need to get out of this office. I run my hands through my hair aggressively, making a mess of it. I push my chair away from my desk, stand up and gather my purse and laptop bag. I swear to God, if I don't ever type another word, it'll be too soon.

Who knew when I took this job right out of college, writing for our local newspaper that I'd end up writing the whole thing myself? I swear there are other people who work here, I'm just not entirely sure what they do. I know Jerry, who runs the paper, is too old to do all that I do, which is why he hired me. He likes to pretend he's still fully involved by coming into his office each day and checking up on what I'm writing. He's never once added anything to the docket or taken out anything I've written. I think he's just happy to have somewhere to go every morning. Susan edits everything that I write before it goes to print, but I'm not sure what she does all week while I'm writing the articles. There's a team in the basement that runs the presses and that is one thing I can happily say I have nothing to do with. Susan and Jerry aren't getting any younger, which is probably why I feel like I'm carrying this whole place on my shoulders. It would be so much easier if it was all online. So many small papers have gone that way and Jerry just won't cave. He likes his paper in his hand, he says.

For some reason, this week has been endless. Thank God it's only a weekly paper or I would have run away long ago, but it's still too much for one person. I have to go to the local schools for the youth sports reports, fundraising updates, and any other relevant news. Then I head to the community centre for the adult sports teams' stats. This is also where the Historical Society holds their meetings, so I catch up on anything newsworthy from a hundred years ago that needs to be printed today. These are secretly my favourite pieces to write. I love digging into the old stories of this town. After that, I check in with the mayor and make sure he doesn't have any business he wants added to the fold. Local businesses all run ads or various promotions that they want space for, so I go door to door and check in with them. You would think in a town this small, where Main Street houses all the businesses, it wouldn't take that long. But all of the owners have known me since I was born, and they'd like the news right from my mouth before I print it in the paper. I don't mind serving the news to the whole town twice, in two different formats, verbally and the written word. Nope, I don't mind at all, except I actually do. These people make me want to scream at the top of my lungs, but instead of doing that and giving Jerry and Susan heart attacks, I make my way out of the building to the street.

I lift my face to the sun shining down and revel in the cool breeze that blows my hair back off my shoulders. Fresh air. Sometimes on the days that I'm inside writing, I miss the days that I get to run around town chatting with people. I know, I'm a walking contradiction. I can go from isolated hermit to social butterfly at the snap of my fingers.

It's been a couple days since I've been out to see Mom and Dad, and there's nowhere in Balsam River I'd rather be than at the farm where my siblings and I grew up. The memories feel like they're locked in a vault and only release when I step on the property. Sometimes the flood of memories hurts more than I care to admit, and sometimes they bring so much joy that I can't help but smile ear to ear. I never know how it's going to land but I know Mom and Dad need me, so the fear of the pain won't keep me away. I plan to stop at Liam's on the way and grab coffee for everyone at the farm, which is a nice excuse to check in with him too. We've been closer these last four years than we ever were before. Losing one of us can do that to you, I guess.

Noah and Liam were super close; brothers only two years apart with all the same interests couldn't really be any other way. Like me, with Amy. We were only a year and a half apart in age. We used to do everything together. As kids it was because there was no one else. Mark and Jenna lived just down the road and joined us all on the farm most days, but we were the only kids for a few kilometres, until you made it into town. As adults we had more options, but we stuck together because we were each other's best friend. Noah and Liam were the same; they welcomed Mark as easily as we joined with Jenna. Noah started hanging out with Jack Turner in high school and he quickly became a part of every adventure. Of course, we had no issue with the extras joining our crew we all melded together as one as the years went on. Mark and Amy started dating in high school, got married, and had planned their whole life ahead of them... but that was before.

Liam and Jenna always had a thing for each other but for some reason never acted on it. The Davis' feel like a distant memory to me now. Jenna is gone to university in Toronto. She left right after everything with Amy. Mark headed west with baby Andi and has never been back. Thank God he calls and video calls, so we do get to see Andi growing into a sweet little girl, even if it is over a computer screen. She is all I have left of my sister, so I will take anything that I can get.

Despite those few friends, at the end of each day, it was the four of us on our parent's farm, feeding cows, riding horses, chasing the cows with the horses and just living the best life we could have ever lived.

Until everything changed.

Now it's just the three of us. My brothers are everything to me and I know they'd walk through fire for me if I asked them to. They've wrapped me into their fold, made their duo into a tripod, and it feels like armour when I'm with them. Like I can take on the world. It's almost like the grief and the sadness are just a little less when I know they're carrying it too.

All of these things are why I will continue to check in on them and I will go to the farm to help Mom and Dad with whatever they need. I will keep writing for the stupid Balsam News and I will do it with a smile because I love these people and I love this town. It's worth it to me to put aside whatever dreams I had of being an author, and writing something other than town gossip, to focus on my family. These are my people and I want to be there for them, love them, and spend time with them while we can. We know all too well that tomorrow is not promised to us.

I push through the door of Liam's and smack right into a brick of a man. It feels like I ran into a wall, but I know it's a guy wearing a plaid button up, worn-out blue jeans, and work boots caked in mud. The smell of earth and evergreens filling my nostrils is why I don't even have to lift my face up to those warm, brown eyes to know that I just ran into Jack Turner.

Jack sequesters himself on his dad's old Christmas tree farm, Balsam Trees, most of the time. It's been his farm for years, but I still always think of it as his dad's. He's always been quiet and a bit of a loner. Other than being close with Noah and Liam, I don't think I've ever seen him with any other friends–male or female–though I try not to dwell on whether I would care if I saw him with a girlfriend. I had my chance with him and I couldn't pull myself together enough to take it. The weeks after Amy died are a blur in my memory but the moments that Jack was there to support me, even though I never asked him to be, will always remain as vivid as if it had just happened yesterday.

I hear a soft knock at the door and I look at it accusingly. It's not late, but I have no social life at all these days. People don't stop by anymore, like the world kept spinning even though Amy left it. Mine stopped, while everyone else carried on. If it's not my parents or my brothers, then I haven't seen them in the two weeks since Amy's celebration of life. After her funeral, after Mark took Andria and left us all, we took a couple of weeks to put together a gathering for the whole community to mourn. It was awful, made even worse by Mark being gone, but we got through it and now we're left to grieve alone. It's been four weeks since she died. Andria's four weeks old. What will it be like for her to share her birthday with the day her mother ceased to exist on this earth? My heart breaks for her all over again just thinking about it. God, I miss her. I miss Mark too. He was like a brother to me, and I can't move past how angry I am that he just took off.

Jenna came to the celebration, but she didn't stay, and she looked like she wanted to climb out of her own skin. I hadn't seen her much in the last six months anyway, but I even miss her right now. Mark may have been like a brother to me, but he is her brother, so I can't imagine how she's feeling. So many people are hurting, but we seem to all do it best in isolation. I can't help but wonder if it might help if we did this together. I wonder, but not enough to find out. It's easier this way.

I open the door slowly to see Jack standing on the other side.

I'm not short at 5'9", but I still have to look up at him. He's looking down at me like I'm the sunshine after a rainstorm, and I don't want to think about what that look does to my stomach. His eyes are darker than I remember but his lips are curved just slightly up, almost forming the dimple that I know appears on his right cheek when he's really happy. Oh my gosh, enough, Sara. It's Jack. Noah's buddy, Jack. But seriously, has he always looked at me like this? Does he look at everyone this way? Maybe that's just his face. I really need to get some sleep.

His dark hair is thick and wavy and as usual, just slightly too long. He always looks like he's just missed his haircut. Has he been running his hands through it tonight? He actually does look a little stressed, but maybe that's just the hair. He looks sad. I always forget I'm not the only one who's sad.

Eyes like cocoa, that only appear lighter out in the sun, are not light at all tonight. I shake my head a little to stop my evaluation and try to give him a smile, "Hey, what's up? What's wrong?"

He turns his eyes down like he's studying the grain in the wood floor.

"Nothing, I just wanted to see how you were holding up."

"I'm okay, you didn't have to come over, Jack. You could have just texted."

"No, I needed to see you. You'll never tell me what you need in a text. Shit, Sara, I'm standing in your doorway and you're lying through your teeth, telling me that you're okay."

A laugh actually scrapes out of my throat. Never one to beat around the bush, Jack just tells me how it is. That's always been something I can count on from him. No bullshit. No point in denying the truth he clearly already knows. Before I can even think about it, I let the tears fall as he wraps me in his arms. Just like the day Mark left, he holds me until my sobs subside. Minutes or hours could've passed, and I couldn't tell you which. The familiar scent that is just so quintessentially Jack envelopes me. He smells like the pine trees from his farm and a spring breeze, and it soothes me. At this moment, it feels like maybe things aren't as bad as I've made them out to be in my head. Maybe I will make it through this. Then I feel his lips brush my hair on the top of my head. My eyes widen, and the intimacy of it snaps me out of wherever my head is going. This is starting to feel like more than I'm prepared to acknowledge, so I slowly release him and step back.

I wave my hand in front of my face and then wipe my wet cheeks. "Jack, I'm sorry that I'm such a mess. I promise I won't always do this every time you see me. I won't always be a blubbering mess, I hope. Though, I am making a habit of it."

"Don't apologize, Sara, I'm here for you, whatever you need. Even if it is to snot on my new shirt." He grins now, and there's that damn dimple. Why does that make my stomach do strange things? Just when I think I will never feel anything but sadness and anger ever again, he walks in and has me feeling whatever this is. What is this? I don't even have the capacity to think about it right now.

I push it out of my mind and move to the kitchen. "Do you want a drink? Beer? Water? That's pretty much all I have to offer."

He laughs and shakes his head. "Nah, I'm good. I just wanted to see for myself that you're doing alright."

I try to smile. "Well, I haven't slept for days, or weeks maybe. I don't even know, but I'm fine. I think this is as good as it gets, Jack." He winces at my words and moves closer. He reaches for my hands, but I evade his touch by taking a step backwards. I don't know what this is, but I can't do it. A crease appears between his brow, but he doesn't reach for me again. His effort to make me feel better feels more like he's suffocating me. I don't want anyone's pity, especially not his. I don't want him to see me like this or think that I'm weak. I'm so tired of people feeling sorry for me. I wish there wasn't anything to feel sorry for. I wish this wasn't my reality. Why did she have to die?

"You should just go, Jack. I would rather be alone." I can see his shoulders tense at my words, like he wants to snap back at me, and I wouldn't blame him, but I know he won't. He's too nice, he's too... Jack.

He doesn't retreat like I expected, but he doesn't move any closer to me either. He's looking at me like I'm a caged animal that's gotten loose and could attack at any moment. He wouldn't be entirely wrong. I feel like I've been on the attack for a month. I feel like I've lost myself just as much as I've lost Amy. I don't know who I am if I'm not her sister. How does life just go on after a loss like this?

Don't get me wrong, I am functioning. I get up in the morning and go to work. I check in at the farm after to make sure Mom and Dad are doing okay. I see my brothers most days. Noah is usually at the farm on his days off from the fire station. He's always thrived on being busy, and Dad can always use the help. I usually see Liam when I grab my morning coffee at Liam's Coffee and Books. I don't know how he has been keeping his business afloat while going through this. Thank God I just have to show up, do my job, and go home. There's no doubt my writing is suffering. My heart isn't in the local newspaper stories right now, but that's a problem for another day. If I'm honest, I don't know if my heart was in it before, but now my tolerance for anything less than joy is completely gone. I just don't want to spend another day of my life not living it to the fullest, but at the same time I can't pull myself out of this darkness to actually do it. I just want to wallow and be sad. I've never felt so torn in all my life.

He's still staring at me. His frown is gone but he's not smiling. I rub my face with both of my hands in exasperation. "Jack, please."

He shakes his head. "Sara, how can you ask me to leave you right now when it goes against everything that I know is true? You need someone. You need me."

"No, I don't. What I need is to be alone. I need to grieve and sleep and go to work and carry on. You being here isn't going to change any of that. Trust me, if it would, I would have called you sooner."

I know he means well, but I also don't know where he gets off. I don't need him. I don't need anyone, not anymore. I needed Amy, but I can't have her, so everyone else can just fuck right off.

I'm so tired of hurting. I'm tired of needing someone, anyone, and then having them just leave. If they didn't die, then they're taking off into the night with their newborn, and others are just genuinely lost in their own grief. Either way I am good on my own. I can count on myself.

I tell Jack as much, and he turns back to the door to put his shoes on. He turns around as he steps out into the hallway of my building. "You know Sara? I'm not going anywhere, and I'm not asking anything of you. I just want to be here for you. I don't want anything in return. I'll be here when you realize this is all bearable if you're not alone."

"When? Don't you mean, if?"

"Nope. I said what I said. I'll be here. I'm your friend, and friends show up." With those parting words he closes the door and walks away.

I'm not sure if that was a promise or a threat, and I don't think I want to find out.

I shake my head a little as if to shake the memory loose but there's no use. I've tried to forget the comfort and safety that Jack brought to my life after Amy died. I've tried and failed, so rather than forget, I have just ignored it. Much safer for me than falling head over heels for one of my brother's friends. I try to take a deep breath but that does nothing for me as it only drowns my senses in everything that is Jack.

Despite seeing him in here often enough, I've done a decent job of avoiding him for the last four years. I try to avoid any in depth conversation as well as any physical contact; no hugs or handshakes or high fives, and especially no resting my hands on his chest like I am right now. My fingertips are pressing into him like I'm using him for balance, like I need the support of his broad chest to keep myself upright. I yank my hands away as if he's burned me. I watch as a crease forms between his brows that tells me he's annoyed at my reaction to touching him.

We used to touch each other all the time. In a friendly way I mean, because we used to be friends. We weren't that close, but then for a minute it almost felt like we could be, and then we just weren't. I ruined that. Grief ruined that.

He showed up for me on my darkest days, but they were too dark. I pushed him away harder than I pushed anyone else. His gorgeous, brown eyes and stupid dimple still haunt my dreams. He still makes me feel too much. Sometimes the tinge of regret is there, but then I remember that things have not changed so much that I can allow myself to feel everything that I could for him. I wish this electric charge that I feel around him would piss off, though. It doesn't matter, I can ignore it. Amy is still gone, and I am still here. Alone is a safer way to live. There's less heartbreak that way.

After we lost Amy, all I knew was sadness and anger. When Jack tried to push his way in, he brought light and smiles, dimples and warmth. And I hated it. I wanted to hurt like Amy did, like my mom was without her daughter, like Andi would as she grew up without a mother. If I'm honest, I wanted to die in her place. I just couldn't feel the things that Jack was making me feel. What would that say about me? That I could find joy in anything just weeks after Amy lost her life. After my mom lost her daughter, Mark, his wife, Andi, her mother. And me, I lost my sister, my best friend in the entire world. How could I even think about feeling anything but pain?

He's staring at me like he can read my thoughts. Crap, I hope he can't, what an emotional shitstorm he would bear witness to. I can't even sort through the chaos that is my mind, so I know he wouldn't stand a chance.

I smile weakly. "Hey, Jack. Sorry to run right into you, I need to watch where I'm going, eh?"

With one hand, he rubs his chest where my hands were just touching him, his eyes softening. "No worries. I was rushing out, should've been more careful too."

We both stand awkwardly; a little too close, but somehow not close enough. If I take a step forward I will be touching him again, but the door is right at my back. With nowhere to go but to sidestep him, I do just that, but he must have the same idea. Now we're just out of the way of the door, but still directly in front of each other. God, why is this so awkward? It's Jack. Just Jack.

With a nervous laugh, I walk around him and head for Liam, who's standing behind the counter. My arm brushes his as I pass, and with another apology and warmth spreading through my chest, I move my feet faster before I fall into his arms or do something else similarly pathetic.

CHAPTER

Two

Jack

My chest hasn't even cooled from her touch when she rushes past me and her arm brushes mine. It feels like sparks are shooting down to my fingertips. I want to jump away from her, like she did from me a few minutes ago, but I also want to grab her and pull her in closer. In the end I do neither. I turn to watch her back as she quickly makes her way to the counter. I saw that look in her eye when her hands were on my chest; only there for a split second, but I saw it. She felt what I felt, I'm sure of it. There is this draw to each other like opposing ends of a magnet. There is something more between us. Or there could be, but she's made it abundantly clear she'll never allow there to be more.

I tried to push my way in after Amy died. I knew she needed me. Well, I thought she did, anyway. My mind slides back to just weeks after Amy died, another day just like today, in this coffee shop with the same beautiful woman in front of me.

I see Liam first when I walk through the door. He's behind the counter, looking like a ghost of himself. Liam's Coffee and Books is all that's been keeping him going these last couple of months. If it wasn't for this business and this town I don't know if he'd drag himself out of bed. I scan the tables and chairs looking for Sara's familiar hazel eyes. It doesn't take me long because when I find them, they're focused on me. I smile and give her a signal to let her know I'll be over in a minute. I make my way to talk to Liam at the counter. "Hey man, how are you holding up?"

He smiles but I know it's his fake 'happy for the customers' smile. "I'm alright, Jack, how are things out at the farm?"

"Keeping me busy enough, planting new trees and making sure the mature ones are pruned perfectly for next Christmas. It's a full-time job on its own but I love it. It relaxes me, walking out between the rows of evergreens all day."

"That's great, man. I'm glad we were all able to help you plant those when you were in a crunch to get them in the ground back when you first took over. God, that feels like a lifetime ago now." His voice trails off and I know he's thinking of everything that has changed since then.

Trying to distract him from his grim thoughts, I tap the countertop. "Me too, don't know what I'd do without you guys, but hey, I'm gonna grab a coffee and check in on Sara. Can you grab me a large black coffee and whatever she's having?"

I can see the relief in his eyes to have something to do with his hands and his mind. "Sure thing. She's just drinking black coffee today too. Not her usual but I didn't question her."

I slide my money his way across the counter. "Make her a vanilla chai latte. She'll forgive me for trying to cheer her up."

He smirks at me as he turns to make our drinks. I can't help but gravitate my eyes to where Sara's sitting. She's basking in the spring sunlight that's coming in the front window, reading what looks like a romance if I can guess by the cover. Her eyes roam over the page hungrily, and I'd give anything to have her look at me like that.

Wait, what? Why do I want her to look at me like anything?

I gotta stop thinking about what I think I want or need and focus on her. She's grieving and needs a friend. A friend, Jack. That's it. Does talking to myself in my head make me crazy? No, talking to myself out loud in the middle of a coffee shop would be much worse. I'm fine.

"Jack." Liam sounds exasperated calling my name. Shit, how many times did he call me?

"Yeah, hey, sorry." He passes me our drinks. "Thanks, I'll talk to you later."

"Where were you just now? I said your name three times before you heard me."

I try to be nonchalant; I don't need him knowing I was daydreaming about his little sister. "I don't know, just lost in thought, sorry about that."

"No worries, I get it." He looks a little forlorn as he turns back to cleaning the machine he was working on before I walked in.

I stride over to the table that Sara is sitting at. She always chooses the one closest to the bookcases that line the wall, as if she needs to be as close to them as possible to choose her next read. I set her latte down as I slide into the chair across from her. Her anger from the other night seems to have dissipated, which is a good thing.

She looks up from her page and smiles. "Hey." She lifts the paper cup to her nose to inhale the scent of the spices before she takes a sip. "Thanks for this." Her eyes close and I can't help but smile when I see her lips curve up a little as she savours the flavour. Who knew a vanilla chai latte could have this effect on her? And on me.

I point to the mug beside her book. "What's with the black coffee?"

"Oh, I don't know, I guess I was feeling miserable and wanted to stay that way."

I frown. "Sara, I know it's hard–everything has gotta be so hard right now–and I won't claim to understand, but if it's too hard to make yourself feel better, then let those around you give it a try. You have so many people that care about you."

"I know, Jack, I know. I can't make it make sense to you. I do want to feel better. It just feels so impossible right now. I want to just sit here and get lost in this story." She flips her book up in the air. "And I want to pretend like this is all that matters, okay? Can you just let me do that?"

"No, I don't know if I can let you do that. I care too much. I can't stand seeing you this way."

She leans in across the table, only inches from my face. Her teeth are gritted and she has steel in her hazel eyes. The green that slashes through the centre is brighter than I've ever seen. "It's not about you, Jack. It's about me, and my sister, and how she's not fucking here anymore. You don't get to make me feel better just to make yourself feel better. Now, please leave me alone." She only pauses for a few seconds before she picks up her latte and her book and heads down the hallway that I know leads to Liam's office.

That escalated quickly. I try not to wince as she storms away. I want to question the hot and cold I've been getting from her, but I know it's no coincidence that she's only been like this since losing Amy. She's a fraction of herself now, but I don't know how to help her find herself again. She's wrong about me though. I'm not just trying to make myself feel better. I guess I can see how she'd think that, but that's not what's happening here. I'm a little insulted that she thinks so little of me that she can't imagine that I might actually care about her.

The memory still stings. My sister says my 'fixer' tendencies are a trauma response.

Fuck that, I don't have trauma.

Okay, maybe I do, but if I do then she does too. Although she'd say she 'processed hers in a healthy way by seeing a therapist for years and working on her relationships and communicating her emotions'. She thinks the answers lie in talking about her past and what she wants for her future, and sharing both with people that are important to her. In her opinion, I let mine fester, seclude myself on my farm, stuff everything inside, and cope by fixing anything and everything I can find that's broken.

Yeah, we've had this conversation a few times.

To be fair, she's not wrong. I do all those things, but it works for me. I don't think therapy is for everyone and it's not like I'm suffering. Seriously, if my worst trait is that I like to help people, aren't I doing alright?

The memory of the day isn't complete without repeating in my head over and over what Liam said to me after that encounter with Sara. He'd told me to walk away.

I'm still sitting at the table that I had been sharing with Sara. I'm sure I look stunned, but I can't bring myself to care. How can I get through to her that I just want to help? I don't want to see her crash and burn like I know anyone could after such a huge loss. Liam walks over and takes the chair across from me for his own.

He crosses his arms over his chest and shakes his head a little. His eyes are cast down like he can't even look at me. "Don't take it personally, Jack, she's hurting so much right now. We all are."

My chest physically aches to think of the pain they're all feeling. I speak softly, "I know, Liam. I know. That's why I'm here, trying to ease it for her and you and Noah. I care about all of you like you're my own family, just tell me what I can do."

"There's nothing you can do. Absolutely nothing. I hate that as much as you do. I'd say be there for her, but clearly she doesn't even want that. I don't know what to say. I can't speak for her, but I want to tell you she'll let you in eventually. This heartbreak is like nothing we've ever felt before, and I have a feeling mine isn't even close to what she's feeling. I think you just have to wait until she realizes she needs you."

"What if that never happens?" I turn slightly in my seat to look towards the hallway that Sara escaped to. I turn back to Liam and notice him watching me now.

He stands and says, so quietly that I almost miss it, "Then you walk away."

I tried to talk to her about it a few more times over the months following that day. When she didn't let me in, I stopped pushing her to lean on me and open up to me, but I didn't *walk away,* not really. I'm still right here. Life went on, the farm keeps growing, more and more people are coming from further away when the Christmas season comes around every year. I catch a beer and a ball game with Noah and Liam when we all have the time. Sara is still right here. She writes for the paper and seems to love running the show over there. She spends all her free time at her parent's farm or hanging out with her brothers. She seems happy, at least whatever happy is after you lose your sister and best friend. I'm not dumb enough to think she's okay, but for lack of a better word, I think she's doing okay.

It's not the first time in all these years that I've thought this, but as I leave Liam's and make my way down the sidewalk to my truck, I can't help but wonder where I went wrong with her. I know how grief changes people; I know we all process things in whatever way works for us, any way that helps us get out of bed in the morning. I just don't know how I can reach her, granted, I'm more than a little out of my depth. I've been with women, but I've never had a serious girlfriend. I've never brought anyone home to meet my family because there's never been a woman that I thought I wanted to share my life with.

I didn't always think that woman would be Sara, but I do now. For years she was just Sara Ryan, a great person, a friend, Noah's sister, but a switch flipped inside of me when I had to watch her break. When she fell apart before my eyes, she felt like she'd lost everything, and I couldn't do a damn thing about it. It goes beyond wanting to be helpful, or wanting to 'fix' things for her, this is a deep, visceral need to make her mine. I am constantly aware of her presence in this town, her helpful demeanor, her quiet but cheerful laugh. Every word I read in the Balsam News feels like she's telling me her stories to my face. She's constantly trying to be everything to everyone; the town, her brothers, her parents, and now Andi. I love that her heart is always in everything she does, but I want to hold her heart in my hands. I want to give her a break from being everyone's person, time to just be and to feel that same love she spreads to everyone she comes in contact with. I want to run my hands through her long hair, massage her shoulders until she melts into my touch. I want to make her smile and laugh and when I can't, I want to be the one to wipe her tears and hold her in my arms.

I've known pain and loss and I thought I could navigate hers, or help her come through it on the other side at least, but she would never let me in. She won't give me the chance to be there for her or help her in any way. I don't know *her* pain and loss, and I can admit that. I never tried to tell her I knew what she was going through, because no one knew or knows, even now. My mom died when I was a boy. I was five, my sister, Kristin, was three. It was sudden, an aneurysm. One day she was there and the next, she wasn't. We grieved her, of course, but it's different when you don't know what you're missing. I remember her a little, but I don't know what it would've been like to grow up *with* a mom, so I don't get too worked up about the fact that I don't have one. What I do remember brings me happiness. I remember her presence; joyful, beautiful, and always smiling. I just focus on the good and it gets me through, but I know it's not for everyone. I've had to watch Kristin struggle to figure out growing up and becoming a woman without her mom. I know it's been tough on her and maybe always will be, for me it's like I wish she was here, but then it ends there.

I have always made sure to be there for Kristin whenever she needed support. I've helped my dad carry on with life since as far back as I can remember. He didn't know the first thing about raising two small kids, so we went to school and worked the farm with him. I did everything I could to fill in his gaps, including buying Kristin her first tampons and giving her boyfriends the third degree when they came to the door before a date. Dad did his best, but at the end of the day he was just spent. He stretched himself too thin and didn't accept help from the amazing community we are a part of. If it wasn't for them, I couldn't have pulled the farm back from the trenches that dad was burying it in. He only wanted help from me, so I gave it, but I learned young that we didn't ask for help from outside the family. Our town made it easier to do when I had no other choice, but he wasn't happy with me after that. Dad lives in a nice retirement villa in town here while I live in the farmhouse that I grew up in, just east of town. Kristin moved to Alton for nursing school and made her home there when she got on full time at the local hospital.

I slide into the driver's seat of my pickup truck as my phone starts ringing in my back pocket. Her ears must be burning because it's Kristin. "Hey sis, what's up?"

"Hey! I'm just heading home from my night shift that turned into a day shift. I just wanted to call and check up on ya before I head to bed."

I chuckle. She acts like she's my big sister, not my younger sister. "Thanks for the check up, but I'm good, just heading back to the farm to finish up the afternoon pruning. It's been pretty warm for May so I want to get them all done before month end, which is keeping me busy."

"Heading back to the farm? Where've you been?"

"Just got in my truck, was grabbing a coffee at Liam's."

I can hear her mischievous smile when she says, "Oh nice. See anyone interesting in there today?"

I know she's digging for information about Sara. I can't mention Liam or Noah without her fishing, thinking there's some hidden love affair going on. I said I walked away; I never said my sister did. I sigh and shake my head, even though she can't see me. "No, Kristin, I didn't see anyone out of the ordinary."

Being vague never works with her. "Sara's ordinarily there, was she there today?"

Shit. She knows I can't lie to her. "Yes, she was there. She ran into me on my way out actually, she was rushing in."

She croons a ridiculous noise implying high school romance. "Ran into you? Did you save her from impending injury, from falling flat out on the floor in front of you?"

"Jees, Kristin, give it a rest. It was awkward as hell, and I don't know why. She acts like I'm the plague and it's been this way for years now. If I haven't broken down her walls yet, I'm never going to."

Now she's the one to sigh at me. "Jack, you're not even trying! You act like you're on this heroic mission and keep failing. You tried to support her in the worst time of her life and she couldn't see you through her pain and grief, so you gave up. You said yourself, it's been years. Get your ass back in that coffee shop and ask her on a date. Tell her how you feel. See how she's doing. How she's really doing, not just how it looks like she's doing. God, Jack, grow a pair already!"

Holy shit, I just got told off by my baby sister. The bigger problem is, I'm not entirely convinced she's wrong. Maybe I should go back in there and talk to Sara. I mean, *really* talk to her.

I almost forgot Kristin was still on the phone, waiting quietly for me to catch up. She groans. "Get there faster big brother."

I laugh because I love that we know each other so well. Even living an hour away, she's my best friend. She knows me better than the guys ever could and loves me unconditionally the same way I love her. Still smiling from her tough love, I say, "I'm there, I hear you. I'll go back in."

All I hear is high pitch squealing and then, "YES! Byeee!" She's insane but I love her. Still shaking my head, I get out of my truck and head back towards Liam's. As I make my way to the door, I can see Sara already sitting in her favourite corner chair, tucked in by the window, with the row of bookcases on the opposite side. There used to be a table for two in that same spot, but she sat there so often reading her book that Liam eventually swapped it out for an oversized round chair that swivels. It suits the shop and that corner perfectly. It suits Sara. With her focus solely on whatever book she's reading she doesn't notice me walk by the window or come in through the door. She barely notices when I'm standing right in front of her. I grab a chair from a nearby table and spin it around so it's facing backwards and set it in front of her big, cozy chair. I take my seat and fold my arms loosely over the backrest, hopefully looking way more nonchalant than I feel. Finally, she looks up.

"Jack. What's going on? Everything okay?"

"Of course, yeah, I just wanted to talk to you, do you have a minute?"

Her cheeks flush pink. I'm not sure what that's about but I think I like it. She responds hesitantly. "Yeah, I guess. I mean, I'm on my way to the farm to see my parents." I raise one eyebrow with a smirk, while glancing at the book in her lap. She looks down to the book and her cheeks turn from pink to red. "I just had a rough day and wanted to take a minute to decompress, but I am heading there after."

I can't help my smile from spreading across my face, I want to be mad that she'd rather avoid talking to me, but her avoidance and defensiveness is kind of cute right now for some reason. I think I mostly enjoy having any kind of effect on her. She scowls as I smile. I better make this quick before I lose her. "I won't take much of your time, not right now anyway. I'll settle for some of it at a later date. Will you meet me for dinner Friday? Come over to my place and I'll cook." I see her tensing up at my words and I'm not above begging so I add, "Please, Sara."

She turns her head so that her gaze settles on something out the window. I never know what the right move is with her, but I'm taking Kristin's advice and I'm going to tell her how I feel.

"Sara, I want to spend time with you because I care about you, and it's more than just caring because you're Noah's sister. I want to get to know you better, for you, and learn who you are and what makes you tick. I can feel that there's something more here and I know you feel something between us too. Don't you want to explore what this is?"

She hasn't let her eyes stray from whatever she's focused on outside, but I can almost see the wheels turning in her beautiful head. She's scared of this; I can see that so clearly right now. I can see it in the way her fingers are tapping rapidly against the cover of her book, and the set of her jaw, tight as if she's restraining herself, but I need her to admit these feelings or deny them outright. I didn't consider the idea that Kristin is way off base and my instincts have failed me. I shake my head as if that will clear those thoughts. She finally turns to face me, her eyes shining with something I can't quite name. Hope, or curiosity maybe. She's quiet for so long that I contemplate just slinking away and hoping she'll believe she imagined this entire encounter but then she finally says, "Okay."

"Okay?" I want to hide my shock and disbelief but it's difficult. "Okay? You'll have dinner with me?" I feel like a teenager asking the hot girl to the prom. I probably sound like that teenager too, but I don't even care.

She picks up her book and slides it into her giant purse and stands from her chair to leave. Before she does, she smiles, just ever so slightly, right at me. "Sure, Jack, I'll see you Friday."

I feel like lightning has struck me right in the chest. I don't know if it was her words, telling me yes, finally, or if it was that smile. God, that beautiful smile. She doesn't know the whole world stops and stares when she smiles. If she did, surely, she would do it more often.

CHAPTER
Three

Sara

What have I gotten myself into? Why did I say yes to him? That damn dimple, that's why. Frig, he is so damn good looking, his hotness blocked all my decision-making abilities. That little speech he made didn't help either. Hot and sweet? Honestly, what was God thinking when he made him and then placed us in the same town? I had grabbed the tray of coffee for the farm from Liam's hands and bolted out the door. Liam's little smirk told me he didn't miss my exchange with Jack, but I don't know what his thoughts about it are. Does he think this could really be something? Jack and I, for real? I don't even know what I think about it, but I should probably let Noah in on the fact that I just agreed to a date with one of his closest friends. He acts like he's the easy going, happy-go-lucky brother but I don't know if that'll stand when I tell him this. I don't even know what made me cave. His vulnerability was so sweet and sometimes I get tired of being the bitch. And I don't just mean to others, to myself too. He makes me smile and when he looks at me it feels like he sees the real me, not just the busy, miserable vibe that I put off. I don't know how he sees through that front. It's almost always stronger when directed at him. Maybe I can have a nice dinner with him and just be Sara.

I lift my hand to knock on his door as it opens to a view that I know I could get used to.

Jack.

Worn blue jeans and plaid button ups never get old when they're covering his body, clearly built from working outside on this farm his entire life. He's not ripped like some guys are from hours in the gym, but has a normal amount of muscle that settles so perfectly under my gaze. I can't deny there's a physical attraction here, but as for the rest, I don't know what it is, or how I feel about it. He snaps me out of my thoughts by touching my hand gently with his own and saying softly, "Hey," and then a little more confidently, "Come in."

It takes everything in me not to yank my hand away. The sparks and heat that come from his touch... What *is* that? Instead, I try to smile and come up with something to say to him. Why is this so hard? I've known Jack for most of my life. But I've never been to his place without Noah, and even then, it was just to pick something up or drop something off. I didn't waltz into his home and sit down to dinner.

It's Friday night and I'm standing on the huge porch that wraps around his century-old farmhouse at 6 p.m. right on the minute. He texted me yesterday to make sure I was okay with chicken alfredo and salad for dinner and to tell me that he'd expect me at six. I'm such a loser, couldn't be a minute early, definitely couldn't be late, had to be right on time. Anxiety is a funny beast, and it's rearing its head again because I cannot form words into a sentence right now. To demonstrate how much he fries my brain cells, all I come up with in response is, "Hey."

To my credit, I am able to get my feet moving. I follow him into the foyer, which opens up into a huge great room that leads further into the back of the house where I can see the kitchen. It looks ridiculously clean and tidy; white, pristine cabinets and stainless appliances scream 'modern kitchen'. It's nothing like I expected to see in this rugged outdoorsman's kitchen, making me realize there's so much I don't know about this man. Now I find myself wondering what it would be like to know him better than anyone else.

After I take my boots off at the door, he leads me through the great room. It's massive, but two huge, cozy-looking sofas and a big recliner fill the space, and a too large, live edge coffee table is centred among them. The table is bigger than my dining table, so I can see why he hosts the guys for game nights. The biggest TV I've ever seen is fastened on the outside wall, bracketed by two huge floor-to-ceiling windows, like old farmhouses always have. I've barely stepped in the door, and I can say already this house is freaking jaw dropping.

"Your home is beautiful, Jack." His steps falter and he turns back to look at me. The shock on his face is telling. Either I don't pay him enough compliments, or he is truly unaware of the beauty surrounding him. "Did you decorate it this way? It's so sleek. Modern yet simple in a way that feels aged like the house."

He smiles, that damn dimple again. I'm not swooning, I'm not swooning.

His deep voice is enough to fray my nerves completely, or soothe them if I let it, but I can't go there, not yet. "Yeah, I did. Thanks, that's exactly what I was going for. It was pretty... let's say, rustic, when my dad was here. I wanted to make it my own."

He leads me to the kitchen, where there's a small table in front of a beautiful bay window that overlooks the farm. A perfect view of the barn just to the left of the house where their animals used to live when we were young, and then rows and rows of evergreens beyond it. The table is set perfectly for an intimate dinner for two, placed right where the sun would shine on it in the morning. Is this where he eats his breakfast? Does he have dates here often? How many women have been in his home and sat at this table? Oh my gosh, Sara, get a grip.

Jack interrupts my mental spiral again, his brow furrowed. "Is everything okay?"

I sputter a little. "Oh yeah, definitely! I was just admiring the view."

He chuckles lightly. "You looked like you wanted to attack someone. You don't like the view of the farm?"

I can feel my cheeks flush. If he wasn't always watching me, he wouldn't have seen my wistful smile transform into jealous rage thinking of other women sitting here. I have no right to those feelings anyway. I have zero claim on Jack Turner.

"My mind just wandered. Sorry, it tends to do that. All good though." I wave my hand towards the table, a huge pot of fettuccine alfredo in the center waiting to be served. "This looks delicious! How'd you know pasta is the way to my heart?"

His eyes widen in surprise, but quickly turn cheeky. "I didn't, but I'm making a mental note of that now."

Laughter bursts out of me. This guy, seriously. "Look at me, giving you tips to help your case."

He mocks being hurt. "Hey, my case is strong on its own, but I won't turn down any help. I'm not just good looking you know, I've got brains too."

I shake my head as I take my seat across from him, feeling completely at ease. The food is amazing, and the company is pretty great too. Jack is an incredible cook, which I would be adding to my list of things I liked about him. He has a cold beer ready for me, knowing I'm not much of a wine girl. *Be still my heart.*

This is everything a girl could want on a first date, except even better, because there aren't any awkward 'get to know you' questions. Jack already knows my family, my job, my childhood, and my grief. We're able to skirt that particular topic, thankfully. Instead, we talk about his farm, his dad, and Kristin, who is working and living in Alton. I love how he lights up when he talks about her, so proud of her and her accomplishments. We then talk about my brothers and my parents and their farm.

I can admit, I'm having a really great time. Jack makes me feel important, cared for, listened to. But at the same time, I can't imagine ever opening that door to my soul for Jack. A part of me wants this with him so badly, or at least the chance to explore it and see what it is and where it could go. But the rest of me knows the heartbreak that would follow would break me, likely into a million pieces. I've been there, and I can't go back. I won't. I'm not even sure I would consider myself whole as it is. There are definitely pieces that shattered beyond repair when my sister died four years ago. I will do everything in my power to protect what's left of my heart, and the only way I know how to do that is to keep anyone else from breaching the wall that I have erected.

CHAPTER
Four

Jack

I can't stop thinking about her. Again.

Fuck! How does this woman do this to me? It feels like I'm back in time. Right after Amy died my thoughts weren't full of Amy, but Sara. I wanted to be there for her more than anything, and then it slowly morphed into wanting more from her. I couldn't stop thinking about her. This isn't quite the same though; this time is better because she's not drowning in grief, she doesn't need saving. She needs attention, care and love, someone to dote on her and worry about her. This isn't like before because this time, I'm going to convince her that we could have something special together. I want to do all of those things for her, and I want them in return. I don't want to save her from anything, except maybe herself. She keeps her heart locked up tight but I'm confident I'm changing that. Slowly but surely, she's letting me in.

Dinner with her was a dream, having her in my home, talking with her about everything and anything that came to my mind. It brought so much peace into my kitchen and to my heart, it felt like everything was finally exactly as it's supposed to be. I'm not particularly talkative, but I found I couldn't stop myself from sharing my thoughts with her. I want her to know me. I can feel this soul-deep connection with her, and I can't let it go.

I'm headed to Liam's this morning to grab her favourite, a vanilla chai latte. I'll take it to her at work and ask her to come to the Spring Festival with me next weekend. The third weekend in May is a national holiday, but Balsam River uses it to celebrate warmer weather and the growth that inevitably comes with spring. Summer is too hot, and we've already got an annual fall fair, so the town fills the gaps with the Spring and Winter Festivals, not-so-creatively named by our town council. The council does a lot for the town and the businesses operating here so we won't judge them too harshly on their lack of naming skills.

The Winter Festival is the only one I have any use for, as it brings tons of out-of-towners into Balsam Trees. Okay, my dad isn't getting any creativity awards either. In my defense, I didn't want to change the name of an established business, however poorly it may have been doing. It was well known to the locals even back when I took it over, and adding pre-cut trees, hot chocolate, and cookies in the old barn has really grown the clientele and attracted people from outside of Balsam River. Everyone loves to attend the festival, then come to me to choose their Christmas tree, have some hot chocolate, and freeze their asses off all in the name of tradition. I'll take anything that boosts awareness of the farm, and that's what the Winter Festival does. This is the first time I've ever felt like I might enjoy the Spring Festival. I'm starting to think with Sara by my side I could be enjoying a lot more of this small-town life.

My eyes and my body are like magnets toward where she's sitting, happily reading in the corner. She's not at work again. That's unusual, but I'm happy to join her for a coffee and ask her about the weekend. I head toward the counter; Liam is behind it talking quietly with a woman I've never seen before. He looks to be showing her how the various drink machines work, as she smiles and nods her head enthusiastically. Must be a new employee. That's great news for him; he's been both running the place and trying to work the counter for a long while. He's earned a break, and hiring a couple more people will give him that.

I hesitate but decide to interrupt because I don't want to waste time I could be spending with Sara. "Hey Liam, can I get a coffee, black, and a vanilla chai for Sara?"

Liam winks at me like he knows what I'm up to. I'm happy to see he's light-hearted about it. Come to think about it, he hasn't been light-hearted about much of anything in a long time. I decide to throw caution to the wind and see what he's thinking.

I nod my head to the side and back, towards where Sara's sitting. "You okay with me winning her over?"

He barks a laugh. "If you think you can, buddy, all the power to you. She deserves all the happiness in this world. If you can soften that heart of hers and give that to her then you won't get an argument from me. Or Noah. If you're worried about that, don't be. She's got tough armour though, Jack. You'll have your work cut out for you."

I smile with relief. "Well, she had dinner with me last night, so that's progress."

Liam's shock is palpable and boosts my confidence even more. With both brows raised he says, "She did? For real? Wow, that's crazy man. I mean, it's great, but crazy."

"Right? I'm going to ask her to go to the Spring Festival with me." I can't even mask my excitement at the prospect of spending more time with her. "We had such a good time last night. She's so great, she's kind and thoughtful and fucking beautiful—"

Liam cuts me off, laughing harder now, "Okay, okay, that's enough, yes she is all those things, now go win her heart and make my sister happy again."

The woman behind him sets our drinks on the counter. Liam turns towards her and says, "Sherri, this is Jack Turner, a buddy of mine, and a regular here. Easy order for you, always a large, black coffee."

Sherri gives me one of the biggest smiles I've ever seen and reaches her hand across the space between us. "Nice to meet you."

I shake her hand and mumble, "Likewise."

She winks at me, then gives her green eyes a little flutter like she thinks she may get more from me. She obviously missed that whole conversation I just had with Liam. Oh well, she'll see soon enough that I'm the most unavailable guy in this coffee shop.

I swipe our drinks off the counter and make my way over to where Sara is sitting. The frown she gives me as I bring a chair over knocks me off the cloud I'd been riding since last night.

"Hey! Got you a latte," I say as I pass her the paper cup that contains her favourite pick me up. She looks at it for a moment before slowly reaching for it. Why is she looking at it like I might have poisoned it?

"Everything okay? You seem a little off."

In a clipped tone she says, "I'm fine. Thanks for the latte."

She casts her eyes back down to the book she was reading before I approached her. Is that a dismissal? What the actual fuck is going on?

"Sara, is something wrong? I had a great time last night and wanted to ask you if you wanted to go to the Spring Festival with me next weekend. Now I'm a little confused. Why are you giving me the cold shoulder?"

She groans without looking up from her book. "I can't do this right now, Jack."

I don't mean to, but I snap at her. "When can you then? Tomorrow? Next Tuesday? Can I make an appointment for some time next month?"

She looks up at me with a fire in her eyes that I haven't seen there in years and she snarls. "How about some time when I don't have a splitting headache from a shit morning at work? Oh right, that would mean never because that's every damn day! Jack, I'm sorry, but this," she flutters her fingers between us, "is never going to work. I'm sorry if I gave you the wrong impression last night, but that's all I have in me, one dinner. I don't want more than that."

I can't even focus on all the other crap she said, because I'm stuck where she admitted every day at work is shit for her. Since when? "What do you mean? Are you not happy working at the paper?"

"No!" Her eyes widened, realizing she's said more than she meant to, "I mean, yes... Well, not really, but it's fine. Ugh! Will you just go and please stop asking me questions?"

She looks exasperated now, but I level my gaze on her, looking into her eyes. I focus on that spray of green that always catches my attention. I make sure she won't look away before I whisper, "Never. I will never stop trying to get to know you. I want in, Sara, and one day you'll open that door and I'm going to be right here on the other side of it. Waiting."

Three Years Later

CHAPTER Five

Sara

"Andi!"

"I'm coming, Auntie Sara! I just had to grab my book!"

Of course she did. I can't blame her, she definitely got that from me, but we need to get going. My mom is waiting for us at the main house, and I need to drop Andi off and get to work before I run out of hours in the day... again. I haven't been back to work for long and I naively thought I could get everything done while she's at school during the week, but the days are so much shorter than I'm used to. So here we are, running like crazy, on a Saturday.

"I'm ready!" Andi bounds down the stairs and plows right into my legs. I grab the door frame so I don't fall on my ass. Laughing, I rest my hand on the back of her head to gently guide her out the door. "Okay sweetie, let's hit the road. Gram is waiting."

She swings the screen door open and runs to my Jeep and buckles herself into her booster seat. Even though we're just going a few minutes across the farm, she knows the rules. I don't have to go on a public road to get there, but after everything... always seatbelts.

The Ryan Family Farm spreads two hundred acres and my brothers both have homes on the property. Liam's is way on the other side–the guy likes his space–but Noah built his a few years ago, right beside the one I'm pulling away from, Amy and Mark's. Mark played right into Noah's dream when he came back a couple of years ago to raise Andi in the house that he and Amy had built. Noah wanted them to live side by side, raise their families together, and spend their nights hanging out here on the farm. It was everyone's dream come true when Mark finally came back, only to be shattered a few months ago when he too was stolen from us much too soon. A car accident during a brutal winter storm on New Year's Day snatched every plan for the future that any of us had. This poor, sweet girl was left an orphan in the blink of an eye. My chest tightens as I look at her beautiful face in my rearview mirror. She's smiling out the window as we pass the mares' fields. I can hear her whispering, "Hi Mama Suzie, hello Mama Red," saying hello to all the horse mamas. She's the sweetest little girl with the biggest heart and I have no idea how she perceives this world to be so bright after losing both of her parents in her short life of seven years. How does she still wake up every morning with a smile, so happy to see the horses and her Gram? Children are so resilient, and I will never not be jealous.

Amy had told Mark that she wanted me to be Andi's guardian should anything ever happen to them. That was before Andi was even born, before Amy died giving birth to her. Before Mark's car accident, before I realized life is fragile and no one is immune to life-changing catastrophes and soul-wrenching grief. Now I have this beautiful, sweet, almost seven-year-old that I'm responsible for keeping alive every day. Not to mention helping her grow into a happy, healthy, well-adjusted human. So many curse words want to spill from my mouth when I think of how badly I'm probably screwing this up, and how much worse it can get as she gets older. These days 'fudge' will have to do, as Andi is attached to my hip twenty-four seven. I smile, remembering Mark always correcting his own swearing in front of Andi. God, how did he do this on his own? How will I ever measure up?

After I drop Andi off with my mom, I skip coffee from Liam's and head straight to the office. I have to get some serious work done today or I'm going to lose my job. Jerry has been accommodating, giving me time off after Mark died, knowing I became Andi's guardian, I would have crashed and burned without the time to get my footing, but I don't think he realizes that I'm not much better than I was a month ago. I still feel like I'm walking around outside my own body, struggling to get through each day, just to find out the next is the same as the last. The local paper still got printed while I took the time off, even though Jerry acted like it wouldn't. I guess when he didn't have any other choice he must have picked up the slack that he's left to me for too many years. Most days I wonder what the hell I'm doing here, why I am killing myself over this job that means nothing to me. But I can't think that way now that I have Andi to provide for.

Mark had a life insurance policy that will more than cover the expenses of raising her, plus her education, but I can't help but feel this pressure to perform, to prove myself worthy of her. Unemployment doesn't look great on the list of reasons to look up to your guardian. Best Role Model Award goes to Auntie Sara! So quitting is not an option. Sherri and Jenna almost had me convinced earlier this year that I could walk away from this place and focus on writing my book.

By that I mean my imaginary book. I'm taking fiction to a whole new level because it doesn't even exist, but I've had ideas for years and always wanted to share my words with the world. It's a pipedream, really, and now I can't even imagine tuning into that creative side. It feels just as broken as the rest of me. I always wanted to spread joy and light through stories of fantasy lands and women winning wars, but now I feel like I've lost the battle. Grief has struck me down a few too many times and survival is my only goal at this point. I will do whatever I have to do for my family, and if that means writing these local ads and gossip pages for the next twenty years, then I guess that's what I'll do.

After a long day at work I rest the back of my head against the wall in the hallway outside Andi's room. She's finally asleep and I wish I could curl up in her bed beside her. She asks for stories about her mom and dad every night and I'm happy to provide that small gift for her, but fuck, it hurts. It hurts so much that they're not here, that they're missing this and she's missing them. I wish more than anything I could take her hurt away. She smiles and laughs but her eyes don't shine like they used to when Mark would tickle her until she had tears in her eyes. He would take her riding on her horse, Daisy, across the farm on all the trails and you could hear her laughter ringing through the air all the way back to the barn. I know we'll find that joy again. I remember the despair I felt after losing Amy, and this is similar, but it's so hard to imagine not feeling this way forever. A knock on the door interrupts my thoughts, probably just as well as I'm about to fall asleep leaning against the wall. I glance out the front window at the end of the hall before I turn to make my way down the stairs. Jack's truck is parked out front beside my Jeep.

I open the door before he can knock again, I say quietly, "Hey, I just put Andi to bed, sorry if you were hoping to see her."

His mouth curves up into a smile, like just the thought of Andi makes him happy. She has that effect on a lot of people, but her uncles are at the top of that list. Liam, Noah, and Jack have really stepped up to show her the type of man her father was and how special he was to them. Jack wasn't always Uncle Jack to Andi but in the last two years since she's lived in Balsam River, he's been a constant for her while hanging out with her uncles and sometimes her dad, so he just adopted the title organically as time went on.

Instead of asking how she's doing, he surprises me. "I thought she'd be asleep, I just came by to check on things, see if there's anything I can do for you."

I roll my eyes. Jack Turner, always coming to the rescue. "Well, you might as well come in, want a beer? I don't have much else to offer other than water or Andi's juice boxes."

He steps in and places his boots on the mat beside mine and Andi's. For some reason, that catches my eye and I think I like the look of them there. I wonder what it would be like to have his boots there beside ours more often, every night, and in the morning.

If it wouldn't look strange to slap myself in the face, I would. What am I even thinking? The loneliness of this grief and single parenthood must be getting to me. How do people do this alone?

God, I must be losing my mind. This is Jack. He's like a brother to me. Except he's not at all because I don't stare at my brothers' asses as they walk away. Damn, his is easy to stare at. Everything is just so easy with him. He makes me feel comfortable and safe and I've almost fallen into that easiness more than once. I feel weak right now, but I need to be strong.

I turn around as Jack twists the cap off his beer and tosses it in the garbage bin. He's looking at me like he knows I've lost it. There's no way he has any clue what crazy-town thoughts just ran through my mind. And screw this anyway, I will not fall apart now. I have to hold myself together for Andi. She needs me.

"What?" I glare at him with a raised brow, "Why are you looking at me like that?"

"Like what, Sara?"

"I don't know, like you think I might fall apart at any second. Or like I already did, and you missed it. Like I'm hanging on by a thread."

"Probably because I know you are. I know you're hanging on by a thread, but it doesn't have to be this way. You aren't alone. Hang on to me, hang on to your brothers. Liam and Noah called me today to see how you were. Why are they calling me? I'll tell you why, it's because you're shutting them out!"

"I'm not. I didn't mean to, I just don't know how to deal with all of this. I'm doing the best—"

He cut me off before my words turned into a sob. "I know, Sara. I know. So do they. We're just worried about you. Don't stand there and tell me you're okay when I know you're not. I know you. I know that you're lost, broken, and unable to see the light at the end of this long tunnel of grief that is consuming you like a disease. I see you. I see you drowning, and I want to help."

I can't stop the tears. I never seem to be able to stop them. Some are for Amy and Mark and for this grief that I can't get out from under, but some are for how seen I feel in this moment. It's like he plucked the thoughts and emotions right out of my head. It almost feels like these tears are washing something away, I just don't know what exactly. I do know that it's freeing to let them fall in front of him. There's a comfort in knowing I can show him all my broken pieces and he won't run in the other direction. He never has. He's always here.

He steps closer. "I'm not going anywhere, Sara. Even if you ask."

I look up into his eyes, so soft and loving. Does he know how to look any other way? I can't help but give in. "I won't ask, Jack. Thank you."

I let him take me into his arms and I let it all out. I don't even care that there's snot and tears mixing on the shoulder of his plaid button up. The smell of pine and earth, mixed with Old Spice and whatever else it is that makes up the smell that is distinctly Jack, is filling me with a peace I haven't felt in weeks.

Why does this feel like home when nothing else in this house does?

Everything here is Amy's or Mark's. I haven't moved any of my things, other than my suitcase that I'm living out of in the spare room. I keep going back to my place to move stuff here but I never end up bringing anything but clothes.

I sniffle. "Jack?"

"Yes, Sara?"

"Will you help me move my stuff from my apartment over here tomorrow?"

He squeezes me tighter. "Yes, love, I can do that."

Andi is with my parents, so I have no excuse to avoid meeting Jack this afternoon to move my things. I have to move. I have to move into Amy's home. Mark's home. Now mine. And Andi's.

It hasn't been Amy's for almost seven years, but it feels like just yesterday that we walked through it together, when they'd just finished the build. I helped her move all her things from the main house and we sorted through her new kitchen gadgets that had been wedding gifts. How was that eight years ago? And now she's gone, and so is Mark. Ugh, this is so hard. For so many reasons. First, that it's theirs, not mine. That, 'not mine' part, pinches my chest tightly. I worked so hard to get off the farm and get my own place and be my own person. Everything has unravelled around me, and I can't seem to stop it. I shouldn't care about petty things like that at a time like this, but I'm an asshole, because I do, I can't help it.

I rest my head against the top of the steering wheel of my Jeep. How has my life come to this? How did we get here? I need to shut down those thoughts as fast as they come, or I'll spiral, and I can't stall much longer; he'll be waiting for me. I slowly get out and make my way to the entrance of my building.

He's standing in front of the main door, like a giant lumberjack sentry. Him and his plaid; if I didn't love it so much, I would laugh. But I do love it, because his predictability is so comforting to me on these days when almost nothing is. Of course, he isn't alone, Noah and Liam stand on either side of him. Again, predictable. As I walk up to them, they all move in with open arms, and despite feeling betrayed by Jack that they're here, I melt into their group bear hug.

"Sar, why didn't you call us?"

Muffled into Noah's shoulder, I replied, "Clearly, I didn't have to."

"You know what I mean. We shouldn't have to wait for Jack to fill us in on what's up."

"I know, guys, I'm sorry. I just don't know up from down right now and didn't want to drag you down with me."

He squeezes me tighter. "Sara! We are all feeling that. Let us do this together. Let us be there for you. We need you too, but we want to be there for you and help you with this stuff." He waves his hand up toward my apartment building. "We can help move your stuff to the farm. That's the easy part."

I pull back, wiping tears from my cheeks. "This isn't the easy part, guys; this is just another piece of me I have to let go of. I want to be everything that Amy was, and everything Mark was, but I'm just not. I won't ever be what Andi needs. She needs her parents. I am not her mom, I'm not anyone's mom! I don't know who I am anymore. I never found myself after Amy died and now it feels like I'm out of time. It feels like all the little pieces that make up who I am are scattered across this countryside. Some days I can't breathe, can't imagine getting out of bed, but that can't be my reality. Andi needs me, Mom and Dad need me, you guys, Jenna, Sherri, you all need me." I'm out of breath after ranting but it feels good to let it out.

Jack steps forward then. "Sar, you're not listening. Everyone needs each other. This isn't one sided. Noah and Liam need you, but they also need to be needed. You need them to get through this, or you won't survive. Shit like this isn't meant to be done alone. We are all here, and we aren't going to let you drown." Liam rests his hand on Jack's shoulder, like a silent thank you for putting his feelings into words.

Noah steps closer to me and wraps me in another hug and says into my ear, "What he said, Sar. What he said."

Pulling apart and wiping tears, we silently make our way up to my place to start loading trucks. Once this is over with, maybe I will see past this darkness and into the future. Maybe there is light in the future, I just can't see it yet.

CHAPTER

Six

Jack

"Andria Amy Davis!"

Oh shit. That doesn't sound good. Who knew aunties can do the 'mom' voice just as well as any mother ever could? I'm currently assembling and disassembling beds in the spare room. Sara wanted her own bed and is putting the extra bed Mark had in here into storage. I hear her storming through the hall and down the stairs to where Andi is watching a movie in the living room. Andi's sweetest voice sounds from downstairs, "Yes, Auntie Sara?"

God, I could never get that girl in trouble. I can see her beautiful green eyes in my mind, her cute little smile as she bats her lashes. I'm such a goner for that girl. Curiosity getting the best of me, I sneak out into the hall. From the top of the stairs I can hear Sara in the sternest voice I've ever heard her use, "Andi, my makeup is a mess all over the upstairs bathroom! Lipstick and mascara on the mirror and counter! What were you thinking?"

She didn't have much to move, so with the four of us loading our trucks, it didn't really take all that long. I don't know how she decided what she was keeping and what she put in storage at the main house of their family's farm. Mark's place was already furnished, so she just had us bring in some pieces she chose to add to what was already here. I didn't know how much of a difference it would make at first, but surprisingly the home already looks like it belongs to her and Andi. It's been Andi's home for the last two years. I know Sara didn't want to add more change and turmoil to her little life, so she decided to move in here with her and make it theirs. She says the little peanut has been doing well, but I can't imagine how alone she must feel after losing her only surviving parent. I can't help but wrap her up in a great big hug every time I see her. Even though she's her regular smiley self again, I know she's hurting.

She'll turn seven in a few weeks, and I know Sara's stressing about making it a good birthday for her. I think it'll be good for them to have this sense of being settled here, together. Kids are intuitive and I would hate for Andi to think Sara has one foot out the door, because she definitely is all in for that little girl and has been since day one.

It almost killed Sara when Mark left town after Amy died, but it was like a piece of her healed when he came back a couple years ago. I can't even think about what these last few months have done to her heart. She keeps it guarded, but she loved Mark like a brother, and I know she loves Andi more than anything. But there's no amount of love that can prepare someone to become a mother so unexpectedly and amidst so much grief too.

A tiny, sad voice comes from down the stairs. "I'm sorry." Andi stops to take a deep breath. "I wanted to draw on my face to be pretty like you do, but it wasn't pretty so I washed it off, but I thought I could leave you pretty drawings on the mirror."

I hear Sara exhale. "How about you help me clean it up and then we can draw pictures on some paper, at the table with *crayons*, how does that sound?"

"That sounds fun. I love to draw!" she exclaimed with a smile back on her face.

"I know you do, sweetheart, but Aunt Sara's makeup isn't for pictures, it's only for my face. When you get bigger, I will share but for right now it's just for me, okay?"

"Okay, I'm sorry I made a mess. I will clean it all up, all by myself!" The last word is drawn out as she gets further away from Sara and closer to where I'm eavesdropping on the stairs.

"Umph—Ah!" Andi shrieks as she unknowingly runs into my arms. I swing her up over my shoulder and climb back up the stairs with her hanging down my back. I set her down at the top and push her back gently towards the bathroom. "I hear you have a job to do. Work extra hard to clean up for Auntie Sara and maybe we'll go for ice cream after."

Her giant smile melts my heart as she runs down the hall to the bathroom to get started. My heart *was* melted until I heard someone clear their throat, very loudly, at the bottom of the stairs. I turn slowly and peer down the stairs at Sara standing at the bottom with her arms crossed. Damn it, she looks pissed. What did I do now? I walk slowly down the steps towards her with both hands up and facing out in front of me. "Hey, I come in peace, what's wrong?"

"What's wrong?" Her voice turns a little shrill, "What's wrong, Jack? How about that I just lost it on my sweet little niece for making a mess when she just innocently wanted to draw for me? How about, I don't know what the hell I'm doing with her, what's acceptable behaviour, and what's acceptable consequences? How about, every time I turn around someone is undoing what I've tried to do?"

She's whisper-yelling all this at me, I'm assuming so Andi doesn't hear, but all I want to do is wrap her in my arms and rub the tension from her neck and back. Something tells me that wouldn't go over well. We've come a long way in the last few years and last week it actually felt like she was letting me in a little. She let me hold her and comfort her right here in this entryway and it was like magic. Even today is a huge step, letting me help her move and to stay to set everything up. She never would have allowed this before we lost Mark. I don't want to know how many times a person can be beaten and battered and broken by grief before they just lie down and quit, but this woman is tough as nails, and she keeps fighting back. If this is the day that I can finally convince her she doesn't have to fight alone, then these seven years of waiting will be worth every second. Instead of wrapping her in my arms like I want to do, I gently place my hands on her shoulders and whisper softly, "Hey. It's okay. You're doing great with Andi. You're everything that she needs right now. Tell me what I did to piss you off and I will fix it."

Her eyes soften ever so slightly when she looks into mine. She blows her long bangs out of her face with a breath directed up at them. Her long hair is tied back in a ponytail today, and several strands have come loose and are hanging down around her face. Those pieces seem to be the lightest in her dirty blonde, and her hair will lighten even more as summer ramps up. She'll be perfectly sun kissed. In a few months I'll have that to deal with again. My summer days consist of trying to resist kissing the top of her beautiful head and trying not to kiss her freckled cheeks every time I see her at Liam's. Fuck, she's so beautiful it hurts.

She breaks those thoughts apart when she splits my heart open by saying, "You undermined me by offering ice cream to do a job I had just asked her to do. I didn't know how to discipline her as it was. I hate taking away anything that makes her happy, even if it cost me two hundred dollars in makeup and created a huge disaster in my bathroom. I felt okay about making her clean it up, but now is she only doing it to get ice cream? Did she even learn that she can't do things like that without asking first?"

Shit! I didn't even think about how my offer for a reward would cause this dilemma for Sara. I don't have a clue what she's going through over here every day, trying to parent this little girl on her own. I want to help her but I'm clueless when it comes to kids and parenting, and now I've made this worse for her.

"I'm sorry, Sara, I didn't mean to do any of that. You were awesome with her. I know I don't know anything about parenting but from where

I'm standing, you're measuring up. I think the problem is you're selling yourself short. You did not 'lose' it on her, you were upset and as soon as you realized it was an accident on her part, you showed her compassion. And yes, cleaning it up is a perfect job for her."

I slide my hands down her arms until her hands are in mine. She looks down at them as if she's deciding whether she's going to grab on or run for her life. I release the breath I didn't know I was holding when her fingers wrap around my hands. I think my heart skips a beat as she says, so softly I almost don't hear it, "Thank you."

I give her hands a squeeze. "I will remind her that ice cream is just because I love her, not because she cleaned up her mess." I don't want to let go before she does, but now we're standing at the bottom of the stairs holding hands looking into each others' eyes and it feels like it could mean way more to me than it does to her. I can't handle the hope that's blooming in my chest, so I slowly release her hands and take a step backward. I point back up the stairs with my thumb to imply I better get back to work, and I turn and start up the steps.

A couple steps up I pause and turn around. She's still standing there, watching me, checking out my ass if I had to guess by the look in her eyes. Not gonna lie, that does something to me. Instead of pushing my luck and calling her out on it, I say, "Thank you for trusting me. I'm glad you told me how you're struggling. Keep speaking up more if people are overstepping. No one knows what they're doing here in this new life. Everyone just wants to help you, Sara, We want to be here for you, and here for Andi. You don't have to let us in, but it will be so much easier if you do."

CHAPTER

Seven

Sara

Liam and Jenna pull in the drive with the promised birthday cake from Kathy's Bakery. "Oh my gosh! Look at it! It's so beautiful!" I say. The cake is a beautiful unicorn, just like the one Andi found on the internet last week. I should've known it'd be perfect because Kathy never lets us down.

Jenna agrees. "I know, right? Isn't it crazy how she can make it look so real? Andi is going to go crazy!" I lean in and give her a side hug so as not to bump the box of precious cargo she's carrying.

"Thank you so much for doing this, guys. She's going to love it!"

Liam steps out from behind Jenna and sweeps me into a bear hug. Do all brothers give the best hugs? Mine definitely do. As I pull away from Liam, I smack his arm lightly and say, "Hey, where's Noah gotten to? He left to get the panels for the ponies' pen forever ago." I point over to his driveway just on the other side of the yard. "His truck isn't back, but it shouldn't have taken this long."

Liam shrugs and looks around as if he might appear out of nowhere. "I haven't seen him, but we came straight from my house. We didn't go by the barns."

"Oh well, I guess he gets here when he gets here. Jack just went over to the Johnsons to get the ponies, so he should be back any minute. They'll just have to stay trailered if Noah isn't here."

"They'll be alright for a few minutes, and then they can run around the corral while the kids oooh and aaah at them. Oh look, there they are now." Noah's truck is coming up the drive from the barns with Jack's following behind, pulling the little trailer.

It's been one hell of a few weeks, and I could really use a nap or a stiff drink, or both. Instead, I'm running around setting up for a birthday party for the sweetest little girl I know. I can't believe she's seven today. A few of her friends from school are coming for an hour while the rest of the attendees will be family. Thank God that Liam and Jenna's drama last week was short lived and had the best resolution we could have imagined. Jenna left town and headed to Sherri's for an undisclosed amount of time. I won't deny it, I lost my shit and ran straight to Liam as soon as I heard. When we lost Amy, Jenna went away to school right after, and never really came back until last fall. She avoided her grief and then had to deal with the fallout when she finally came back, and thankfully found her way back to Liam. But losing Mark really hit her the hardest and I was so afraid her grief was taking over again and that she wasn't going to come back. Not only would I lose a friend that I feel like I just got back, but I could not bear to see Liam hurting anymore than he already was. So of course, he went after her, worked his sweet-talking magic, proposed, and brought back my soon to be sister-in-law. I am so freaking happy for them. I can hardly believe it, but at the same time I can't imagine their story taking any other route.

This family needs some joy right now and celebrating the love that they've found again is so perfect. Andi is beyond ecstatic to be their flower girl and Jenna asked me to be her maid of honour. I am so grateful, but I can't ignore the pang of sadness when I remember that Amy isn't going to be here for our brother's wedding. I always thought I would have a small wedding on the farm one day, that Amy would stand beside me like I did for her on her wedding day. We would raise our kids together, supporting each other, no matter where we landed in this world. I can't even fathom an alternative to that now. I don't have time for a relationship, even if I could handle being that vulnerable again. I'm not blind, I know I have issues since losing Amy, and even worse since Mark. I know my thoughts are unreasonable, but I can't put myself in a situation where I will love someone with everything I have. To do that, just to have something terrible happen, and then having to pick up my broken pieces all over again. My heart can't handle it and besides, my hands are full now anyway.

I'm raising Amy's daughter, trying my best to be a fraction of the mother that she would've been. I'm also trying to not get fired from the Balsam News, even though I hate it there. My priority is Andi and always will be. Jerry knows that, but I don't know if he really understands what that means. No more twelve-hour days or late nights, and now weekends are pushing it too. I know she loves being with my parents at the farm, but I hate that she *has* to be there. Most weeks, she's there more than she's at home and it's not sitting well with me. Amy would've been home with her every day, that was always her plan. It's starting to make sense to me now. Between keeping the house clean, Andi fed and watered, and making sure she gets to bed and school on time, I'm exhausted before I even get to work. She loves spending time at the barn with the horses. My dad and Noah and the hired guy have been riding with her when they get the chance. I've heard now she's made them commit to twice a week and she's labelled them riding lessons. She keeps saying she wants to try ballet and a note came home from her teacher yesterday that she needs a tutor for reading. Apparently, she's not progressing this year like she should be... well, no shit, I wonder why?

Today, I will push all that aside and focus on her special day. It doesn't seem to matter how many years go by, but April 29th never gets easier. Remembering the day that Amy breathed her last breath as her baby took her first will never not feel like a punch to the stomach.

I've been trying to take Jack's advice. I hate it when he makes sense. He offered to help with Andi's birthday party when I said I wanted to have it here at Mark's— I mean, at *our* house, rather than at the main house. My mom means well and only wants to help when she offers to take on these tasks, but it inevitably ends up making me feel inept and I already feel that way enough these days. But a birthday party? That I can do. She was disappointed when I told her I was doing it here, but I think she understood when I told her it was just something I needed to do for Andi and for myself. Even if I don't need to prove myself to them, I need to for me. I need to believe in myself, that I can do this. That I can be the best option for Andi and not just the one her parents chose when we all still thought, 'that won't happen to us.' So here I am, sweating from setting up the inflatable bouncy castle thing, waiting on Jack and Noah to get this pony show on the go. Thankfully the cake is here and Mom insisted on bringing salads to go with the pizza I have ordered for lunch. She's inside setting that up now. It will be everything Andi deserves, and I've managed to let people help me. I can do this. *We* can do this!

"Who's that with Noah?" I raise my hand to block the sun from my eyes as I try to make out who is sitting in his passenger seat, but it's no use. He pulls into his own driveway and parks in front of his garage while Jack backs the trailer up on the grass between our two houses. Why is that so sexy? So the guy can back up a trailer, but why does he have to make it look so effortless? I need to get out of the sun, because it's clearly getting to my head.

Of course he catches me flushed while watching him back up a freaking trailer when he turns back to look at me out his open window. He juts his thumb back to the trailer and then gives me a thumbs up with raised eyebrows, farmer language for "Is that good?" I laugh and nod. It is good and he knows it. I think he knows more than I give him credit for, but I'm still ignoring that.

We can easily unload and lead the ponies to Noah's backyard and not disturb the kids that are already arriving and playing in mine. I glance into my yard to make sure the kids are all accounted for and safe as Jenna squeals and bolts towards Noah's truck. What the heck has gotten into her? As soon as the thought crosses my mind, I see Sherri stepping out of the passenger side of Noah's truck. I had invited her to Andi's party, but I didn't know if she'd come. She didn't say no, but she didn't say she'd be here either. I'm so glad she made it. She had dated Mark for a few months before his accident. They weren't serious in the sense that they were planning a wedding or anything, but it was her first relationship in years and his first since Amy. So no matter their plans or status, it was serious enough.

Her and Jenna built an amazing friendship last year. While Sherri was starting something new with her brother, Jenna embraced the sisterly bond and welcomed Sherri into her life and family. They became inseparable almost immediately. I hadn't realized how much I missed having girlfriends to chat and hang out with until they wrapped me up in their love too. I don't know how I would be making it through these few months if it wasn't for Jenna. Somehow amidst her grief she's still able to be here for me and Andi. I don't know what it's like to lose a brother, but I know the bond with a sibling is like none other. It's unpredictable how much it can shatter you when it's lost. Even though Sherri decided to head back to her hometown to take some time and space away from Balsam River, Jenna is continuing to be an amazing support for her too. Snapping out of my thoughts I smile and wave as I make my way over to them. When I'm close enough that I don't have to yell too loud, I call out, "Sherri!" At the same time, she says, "Sara!"

We laugh as we collide in a long overdue hug. Grief is so strange; it can tear us apart and it can bring us together. I've missed these ladies so much these last few months. They make me forget why I isolated myself, forget why I thought I had to do this on my own. Sherri squeezes me tighter and I can feel tears welling behind my eyes. My breath hitches and I hold on for dear life. This pain never goes away, it shifts, and it makes room for other feelings, and more pain, but it's always there. I pull away from her slowly and wipe beneath my eyes. "Thank you for coming. I know this can't be easy for you."

She smiles, nothing like her usual megawatt smile, but a gentle, loving smile to calm my nerves. "Nothing would keep me from celebrating that little girl." She glances to the backyard where Andi is running around the bouncy castle with her friends. "She's so special, and she deserves all the love in the world."

My heart warms at her words, because she's so right. Andi has so many people that love her, that will always be here to rally around her and celebrate her and lift her up. I have all those same people and it's about time I recognize them, maybe even invite them into my life and my struggles.

Jenna leans in so she's close to both of us and whispers, "How did you end up coming with Noah? Where's your car?"

Sherri rolls her eyes. I'm a little surprised at her tone, but clearly, I'm missing something that Jenna's been on about because Sherri looks more annoyed than shocked. "My car is back at the barn. I came in that way to see if anyone needed help at the main house, but everyone was already gone except Noah loading up the corral. He offered to give me a ride.He said he has to take it all back after the party anyway."

Jenna smiles and I raise an eyebrow, but Sherri just waves us off as she heads towards where Andi is now visiting with my parents at the picnic tables. I turn my questioning look to Jenna. "What was that all about? Something I'm missing?"

She smirks but there's a sadness in her eyes "No, not really. I just want everyone to feel the kind of love I've found with Liam. I may be looking for it where it doesn't exist." She shrugs and looks over to where my family and Sherri and Jack are huddled around Andi, listening intently as she most likely tells one of her crazy stories. "I know they're both hurting so much, and I've seen glimpses of them supporting each other these last months and I love that for them. I know she loved Mark, but I don't want losing him to stall her life. I don't want that for anyone." She turns towards me. "We've already done that once, Sar, don't let it happen again. Don't hide and lose more precious time. There is love right in front of you and you can't keep turning away from it."

My cheeks are immediately warm, although I'm not even sure if it's from embarrassment or a glimmer of anger. I feel a little indignant that she's trying to tell me how to live my life or how to handle my grief. But embarrassment takes the lead this time because in my heart of hearts, I know she's right. I look over to the crowd of my family and friends just as Jack lifts his head, and his gaze pierces mine from across the yard. I can see his eyes shining with love from here. I know he's been keeping his distance, because I'm a bitch and forced him to. But damn it had felt good to be held by him. It would feel so good to be loved by him.

Everyone says grief is love, but if they'd felt this grief, they wouldn't all just walk blindly into love.

CHAPTER
Eight

Jack

I was hoping to make this move three years ago but I never got the chance. I won't let it slip through my fingers again. These two are going to help me this time and I won't be taking no for an answer.

Noah is sitting across from me while we wait on Liam. They've both offered to help me get the mature trees pruned before the weather gets too warm. It's been a hot and dry spring for northern Ontario and that's making it harder to stay on top of my plans of having these trees ready for this Christmas season. I can shape them as I go through the year leading into colder weather, but the pruning should be done by now. There are about four thousand mature trees and thousands more in various states of growth, so the three of us definitely have our work cut out for us. I'm grateful to the guys; they've offered to help whenever they can, and it's turned out to be making all the difference between me sinking or swimming this year. I have more than six times the trees than were here when I took over from my dad almost ten years ago. The numbers were slowly declining each year for him, mostly because his heart wasn't in it anymore. It's taken a long time, a lot of work, and lots of help from the community when times got tough, but I've turned the farm into one of the most successful Christmas tree suppliers in northern Ontario. I ship anywhere in the province and trucks are coming anytime after the first week of November to load up and haul trees to various stores. There's no doubt it's my pride and joy but I'm more than a little tired of it being the only thing that consumes my life. I'm not getting any younger; at thirty-one, I am ready to share my life with the woman I love. If only she'd give me the chance to love her.

The Spring Festival is this weekend and I need to figure out how to get Sara to go with me. If Liam doesn't get his ass over here, we won't even get to the pruning. Winning over Sara is more important and if these two guys can't help me get it done then I don't have a chance in hell.

Noah startles me when he claps his hands together loudly. "Alright, J! What's the plan? Liam's probably lost in Jenna-ville, so we won't see him for hours. Should we get started?"

I nervously rub the back of my neck. I've had some words over the years with Liam regarding how I feel about Sara, and he's always been on board and encouraging, but it never came up with Noah. It never ended up going anywhere with her so there was never a reason to broach the topic with him, but here I am, going in blind. Talk about sinking or swimming.

His brow furrows as he takes in my nervous posture. "What's up, Jack? Everything okay?"

Stuttering, I try to answer. "Uh... ya... I...umm..." 'Try' being the key word there.

Fuck! I'm such an idiot. What is wrong with me? This is Noah, happy-go-lucky, slap you on the back, fun-loving, Noah. Come on. Get it together.

"I want to take Sara to the Spring Festival... I mean, I want to ask her to come with me."

Noah bursts out laughing... and keeps laughing. For a long time. Asshole.

"Okay, fuck off! Is it really that funny?"

Wiping tears from his eyes he says, "Is it really that funny? That you're sweating and bumbling like a shy teenager asking a girl out on a date?

Yeah, it's really fucking funny. Just made my day, my whole week maybe!"

"Okay, okay. I was nervous about talking to you about it, you asshole, not about asking her."

He's still chuckling and shaking his head but answers me seriously. "Nervous about me? Why? You got it wrong; Sara will chew you up and spit you back out. It's not me you should be worried about."

I wince at his words. They hit a little too close to home with what Sara has done to me multiple times over the years. Maybe I'm the idiot who keeps coming back for more.

"I don't know, I just wasn't sure how you'd feel, you know... your friend and your sister."

He laughs again, "Ah shit, Jack, I couldn't care less about that, I'm not friends with anyone I wouldn't allow to date my sister. Hence, I don't have many friends, but I don't make a habit of hanging out with assholes. I know how much you care about her, and have for years. I just don't know if you'll ever win her over. She's not the same as the rest of us. She isn't an open book, she doesn't share her thoughts and feelings freely. She's smart and creative and uses that to shield herself and to deal with things in her own way. She closed herself off after Amy and other than letting Jenna and Sherri into her world, I'm afraid the gates have been locked against newcomers."

"I know." I rub my hands down my face in frustration, "Fuck, I know. Noah, I can't stop trying. I can't help but feel like I'm on this precipice, and I want to jump. I want to see what it's like to fly over the edge. Maybe losing Mark brought her closer to me rather than further away. Is that possible? After Amy she was unreachable, but this feels different. She needs me, and I think she knows it this time."

Liam comes around the corner of the house as I say those last words. He looks between us both inquisitively and then takes a seat slowly.

"What'd I miss? That sounded serious. Who needs you?"

Noah fills him in, and he thankfully refrains from laughing his ass off again. Liam of course is all seriousness. I can always count on him to understand the gravity of a situation.

"So, what do you think?" I ask him, expectantly.

He leans forward in his chair and rests his elbows on his knees, with his hands clasped in front of him. I feel like I'm preparing for a death blow.

"I honestly don't know, Jack. I don't know if she's ever going to see you. You deserve someone who can love you back with everything they have. Sara's my sister and I love her more than anything, but she isn't the easiest person to love. She's worth the battle, I just don't know for sure that you'll win it."

My shoulders collapse in defeat. I don't know if I have the strength to keep fighting for this if everyone and everything is against me. Just when I'm about to give up on this conversation and possibly the woman of my dreams, that I've been chasing for seven years, Noah jumps up from his chair, startling both Liam and I. He rubs his hands together with excitement. "Come on, you two. This is Sara we're talking about! Don't give up on her. I see that look in your eye, Jack. Don't admit defeat, not yet. I'm not ready to deal with another mopey S.O.B, I just got rid of this one." He nods his head towards Liam with a goofy grin on his face.

"What do you suggest? I know we have work to do, but it's more important to me to have your support and any ideas that will help me end this bullshit with her. I want to make her mine and I know I can't do it without your help. You are the two people she trusts most in this world."

Both of their eyes soften, thinking of their little sister and how much she looks up to them and trusts them. I love this family so much and it kills me to think they've been through the worst heartaches imaginable.

"We can get to work, because the first step to getting Sara to spend the Spring Festival with you, is to not even ask her."

I look at Noah like I have no idea what the hell he's talking about. Mostly because I have no idea what the hell he's talking about. "How can I go to the festival with her if I don't ask?"

The glint in Noah's eye tells me he isn't as enamoured by Sara's trust in him as I originally thought. He's planning deception and he's not even going to feel bad about it.

"We'll set her up. We have plans already to all go together. Saturday is always the day we wander the vendors, check out the carnival rides, and then grab dinner together before the fireworks show. *We,*" Noah motions towards Liam, "just won't show up. Perfect day and evening for you two to just hang out. What's she going to do, run away?"

Liam laughs and says, "Hey, don't joke, she's been known to."

I roll my eyes at Liam's joke that's not really a joke. He ignores me and continues, "I'll talk to Jenna, but I know she's going to love this. She's going to be so pissed it wasn't her idea."

"Do you guys think this will really work?"

"It's a start, and regardless of whether it 'works,' she needs to have fun. She needs to see what life can be like if she allows herself the time and space to be herself, *for* herself. She's constantly running around for everyone else, but this day with you, with none of us around, it could be the first time in years that she could allow herself to feel something other than fear and worry."

My hopes are impossibly high right now because what they're saying actually makes sense. It's a little sneaky but they're right. If I ask, she'll say no. I can do it this way, and ask forgiveness later. This is everything that I've been wanting all these years; to spend time with Sara, to take some of the weight off of her heart, but mostly, to just have fun with her. I want to hear her incredible laugh and see her beautiful smile; I want to be the reason the green in her eyes shines brighter.

CHAPTER

Nine

Jack

I'm waiting outside of Liam's Coffee and Books when I hear my favourite voice coming from down the street. "Uncle Jack!" As I turn around, Andi runs into my arms. I instinctively lift her and spin around to hear her squeals of joy. God, I love this girl. To hear her laughing and full of happiness after everything she's been through gives me so much hope for the future. I would give anything to be able to bring her this kind of joy every day for the rest of her life.

"Where is everyone?" Sara's annoyed tone snaps me out of my reverie with Andi.

We all planned to meet in front of Liam's to walk through the festival and spend the day together. Sara's ten minutes late, so she's thinking everyone else should be here by now. She doesn't know that no one else is coming.

I shouldn't be this nervous, but there's no hiding that I am. If Sara finds out everyone bailed on purpose to give me some time with her, she is going to be pissed. I just have to hope that she has a great enough day that it doesn't really matter in the end. Worst case, Andi and I have a great day, and nothing changes for Sara. Then I'll have to face the fact that she may never see me as someone she could lean on, confide in, or spend her life with.

I place Andi back on the ground and she slides her little hand into my much larger one. I look at Sara and notice her eyes are on our joined hands. She smiles so slightly I almost miss it, before her eyes meet mine. I shrug my shoulders. "I don't know where everyone is. I was a little late too; maybe they got a head start. I'm sure we can catch up."

She looks at me pensively. I can tell she's considering her options. I know she feels some of what I feel when we're together. The difference between us is that she's scared shitless of it. She can't avoid me if we start this day out with just the three of us, even if she thinks we'll meet up with the others eventually. But I know they're nowhere near the Spring Festival today. This is my chance. Fighting my nerves and throwing caution to the wind I grab her hand with my free one and say, "You'll survive spending a little time with me today, Sara. What do you think is going to happen?" I don't give her a chance to answer or pull away as Andi and I drag her down the open street that's lined with vendors of all kinds.

"What do you want to look at first, Andi?"

She looks up at me with her big green eyes and yells, "Toys!"

My smile widens. "Of course, duh, what else, right?"

She giggles as she drags us to the nearest tent that is filled with handmade wooden toys and games for all ages. Out of the corner of my eye, I can see a smile slowly creeping onto Sara's face, and her hand is still firmly clasped in mine. I'm winning already.

I didn't know the Spring Festival would be a completely new experience compared to any other year just because I had a seven-year-old in tow. So much walking. Every time I bought her a toy or won her a stuffed animal from the carnival games, she wanted to take it back to the car. I tried to convince her we could carry some for her, but she insisted we all have free hands. She needs us ready and able to each hold her hand to swing her between us when the crowd is thin enough. You won't find me complaining about walking through our hometown with my hands full of these two beautiful girls.

"Okay, peanut, I think it's time we call it a day on the games and buying toys. Let's go find the midway and go on some rides next. How does that sound?"

"Sounds good! Can we go on the Ferris wheel? I love going on that one."

"Of course we can. We can go on it as many times as you want."

Sara tightens her grip on my hand for a second but quickly loosens it and rolls her eyes at me as she asks, "Are you going to spoil her all day? This is crazy."

"I can't help it when she looks at me like that. How do you ever tell her no?"

She laughs and then winks at me, actually *winks at me* and then says, "Spoiler alert... I don't."

I burst out laughing. "You must sometimes! What if she wants chocolate for supper?"

She shrugs. "She doesn't. She never asks for anything crazy. She is such a good kid; the worst trouble we've had is that day she got into my makeup. She does kid stuff like that, but never anything too horrible or destructive. I think God knows I needed to catch a break so He made the easiest kid imaginable for me to raise."

My smile fades as I think of everything she's been through. This incredible woman has survived so much. She's still standing tall, showing up for everyone when they need her, especially Andi. That little girl has been through more than most people in their whole lives, but she is lucky to have her Auntie Sara in her corner. She won't ever fill the hole that Mark and Amy left but she will provide the best life she can for her, with unconditional love and understanding and that's more than a lot of kids get..

"Hey, where'd you go just now?" Sara asks, looking at me with a concerned look that I see her give Andi so often.

"I'm here. Was just thinking about how amazing you are. Have I told you that lately?" I point to where Andi is sitting on a bench devouring her cotton candy. "That girl is lucky to have you. She's really thriving and that's on you. I hope you know that."

Her cheeks flush pink at the compliment and I want to lean down and kiss her, more than anything in the world. But that can wait. Jeez, don't scare her off, Jack. Instead, I clap my hands together and shout, "Who's ready for the Ferris wheel?"

Sara hangs back as we climb the ramp up to the podium that's at the base of the huge wheel. This is something I have in common with Andi, the Ferris wheel is my favourite. I turn around and notice that Sara isn't following and looks a little green around the gills. "Hey, Sar, you okay?"

She blows out her cheeks as she exhales. "Umm... yeah.... I... No, I'm gonna pass on this one."

"What?" I ask incredulously. "You are not *passing* on the Ferris wheel, it's why we're here, Sara."

"It might be why you two are here, but it's definitely not on my agenda for tonight."

Is she afraid of the Ferris wheel? I couldn't have planned this better if I tried. Am I her knight in shining armour that changes all our plans and saves her from the humiliation of being a grown ass woman who can't ride the slowest ride at the festival? Will I be her hero and smooth this over with Andi, give her something even more fun to do so that Sara doesn't have to be embarrassed in front of her niece by being a grown ass woman who's afraid of the FERRIS WHEEL?

No, I am none of those things.

As quickly as I can without drawing her attention, I stride over to where Sara is hesitating, I bend slightly and wrap my arms around her legs just below her ass and throw her over my shoulder. As she's smacking my back with her fists screaming at the top of her lungs, I carry us both to where Andi's waiting to get in the pod that's open for us to take our seats. The carnival worker steps back out of my way and laughs into his fist, trying to be inconspicuous. I think he failed at that because Sara yells, "This is not funny!"

Andi is wearing a smile that I haven't seen in months, one of pure joy. She takes her seat, leaving lots of room for me to not so gracefully plunk her aunt down beside her. "Are you scared, Auntie Sara?" she whispers.

Sara's sitting between us, with red cheeks and a mess of hair on her head–my fault from having her upside down–but damn this look is working for her. She is so gorgeous.

She glares at me, then back at Andi before she says, "No. I am not *scared*. I just don't enjoy being this high off the— ground." She chokes out the last word as she looks over the side of the pod. I take her face between my hands and force her eyes to look into mine. "Don't look down." I use the firmest voice I can muster. Her eyes widen, and I see something flash in them that I've seen once before, only fleetingly, and years ago. She wants me. She wants us. She likes when I take care of her, and the feel of my palms against her skin. I can tell just by that little gleam in her eye. It's gone almost as fast as it appeared, but I have it saved in this memory bank of mine for eternity. It will keep me in this fight for her heart, when I feel like there's no hope. If it ever feels like she will never let down her walls, I will remember that look she gave me just now.

Andi clears her throat and forces me to break contact with her aunt. When I turn my gaze to her, she's staring at us with one eyebrow raised. I smirk at her and give her a wink. She giggles and looks at Sara. "Auntie Sara, you look like you're scared. You should just hold on to Uncle Jack and he will keep you from falling."

Sara swallows audibly, still staring at me. Her eyes drop to my lips, then back up to my eyes. How many times will I have to stop myself from kissing her tonight? I slowly release her face, gently brushing under her chin with my finger. I let my smile spread across my entire face. "Yeah,

Auntie Sara, just hold on to Uncle Jack."

I swear I hear her mumble something about my dimple, but then she turns quickly to Andi and grabs onto both of her hands. "You're right, sweetheart. I am scared, but I have you here with me so I don't need to be. We've got each other's backs, don't we?"

Andi beams with pride, and yells, "Yeah! And Uncle Jack's too!"

Ha! I knew I loved this kid; she is just pulling out all the stops for me today. I don't know if she's old enough to know what she's doing, but I'm here for it.

Sara looks at me over her shoulder. Without letting go of Andi, her lips turn up into the slightest smile. "Yeah, I guess Uncle Jack's too. He's not so bad." Andi giggles and continues chattering about everything she can see from high above the town. I try to focus on what she's saying but I can't take my eyes off the woman sitting between us. Her cheeks are still flushed, and I don't know if it's from being thrown over my shoulder or if she can feel my gaze on her right now. She's avoiding eye contact at all costs, and I don't even care. This woman is fierce and protective and I want more than anything to be the one to protect her but if this is all I ever get; it will be enough. She will always be enough for me.

Before I know it the wheel comes to a stop and we're waved out of our pod onto the platform and back into the festival. I take Andi's hand and then Sara's in my other and give her the full-dimpled grin when I say, "There's nothing like sitting on top of the world with my two best girls!"

I get a chance to look her in the eyes again and I'm startled to see she's not hiding the way that made her feel. The spray of green is shining brightly and her smile rivals mine. I try not to respond like a teenage boy with no control over my body or emotions and instead I start walking, dragging them both behind me.

"How does Cara's sound for supper? You like macaroni and cheese, or spaghetti, don't you, Andi?" I know those are her two favourite foods, so Cara's Italian Restaurant is going to be a hit. It really feels like I can't lose today. Spending the day with these two amazing women is filling my soul like I never could have imagined. I will stop at nothing to make Sara see what kind of family we could be, that I need her, and she needs me. I would give anything if she would just stop fighting it.

As we step into Cara's we hear a loud booming voice calling out to Andi. "There's my girl! Where have you been all day?"

Sara's dad, Brent Ryan–larger than life and just as loud–is leaning out of his chair from a dining table with his arms spread wide ready for Andi to run into. She doesn't disappoint; she's always more than happy to see her grandparents. She missed getting to see them in person for the first five years of her life and she's been making up for lost time ever since. She climbs up on his lap and starts munching on the leftover garlic bread from his plate. Sara tenses beside me and takes a step towards them. I watch her mouth open and then close; she wants to reprimand her but is deciding if she should. I place my hand on her lower back and lean in. I whisper in her ear, "It's okay, he doesn't seem to mind." She glances sideways at me, rolling her eyes and says just as quietly, "He wouldn't mind if she stole the car and drove it through that front window."

I bark a laugh and quickly try to cover it with a cough, so as not to draw attention to us, but it appears to be too late. Brent and Marie Ryan are sitting at their table with Andi and all three of them are watching our exchange with little smiles that tell me even her parents are on Team Jack. Sara rolls her eyes at them now, but I notice she doesn't step out of my touch on her back. If anything she leans into me, just ever so slightly. My pulse picks up as if I've never touched a woman before, but with Sara, it's that I've never touched *her* like this before. She's never let me get close enough for these small intimate touches we've been sharing all day and there's no other feeling in this world like knowing she's letting me in.

"Why don't you ask Auntie Sara if we can have a sleepover tonight?" Marie says to her granddaughter, just loud enough that her daughter can overhear.

"Can I? Can I? I would love that, Auntie Sara, pleeeeaassse," Andi whines with a smile that would rival the sunshine.

Sara squirms a little. How will she get out of this one? She's about to lose her seven-year-old buffer for the evening. "Right now? We haven't even had supper yet, and don't you want to watch the fireworks?"

Brent picks up the small container from their table. "Oh, we have lots of leftovers here. She can have macaroni and cheese when we get back to the farm, can't you, bug? I mean, as long as that's okay with you, Sara."

I can tell they're all struggling to fill the roles they think they should in Andi's life. The Ryan's are used to taking over and being in control and there have been so many things this year that they just couldn't control. They're going to have to get used to Sara being in charge when it comes to Andi, they never would have stepped on Mark's decisions regarding his daughter. If anything, it's more important for them to respect Sara in this role because she's having a hard time respecting herself. As much as I want them to take off with Andi for the night and leave me some time alone with Sara, I want her to feel supported in her role as Andi's guardian even more. So, I take a step forward and say, "Whatever you think is best, Sara." I make sure everyone at the table can hear me. "If you want her to stay with us, we'll have a great time together."

I watch her closely as her shoulders lower and her whole body relaxes. She smiles at me, and then at Andi and her parents. "No, it's okay, go ahead with Grandma and Grandpa and have a great time. I'll pick you up after your riding lesson tomorrow morning, okay?"

Andi claps her hands excitedly and wraps her arms around Brent's neck, Marie says, "Don't you have work tomorrow morning? She can stay for the day."

There go her shoulders, tensing up again. She furrows her brow and says, a little snappier than I've heard all day, "It's fine, I can be back before she's done riding."

What is going on with her at work, that the mention of it has this affect on her? I want to get to the bottom of that but now is not the time. For now, I just stand at her back and support her in any way she needs. Andi hops off Brent's lap and rushes to us both to give hugs goodbye. My heart almost falls out of my chest when she holds my face in her tiny hands and kisses my cheek, then whispers in my ear, "Thank you for making Auntie Sara laugh today."

This kid is going to be the end of me.

Fighting the burn behind my eyes that's spreading to my nose, I give her my biggest smile. "No thanks necessary, peanut. Making your auntie laugh is my favourite thing to do."

CHAPTER

Ten

Sara

My parents just stepped out the door to take Andi to the farm for a sleepover when Cara comes rushing out of the kitchen at the back of the restaurant. She looks flushed and stressed as she rushes to Jack, placing both of her hands on his chest. I feel a twist in my gut that I'm not accustomed to, nor a fan of. Is this jealousy? Why would I be jealous? She can touch him, anyone can, he's not mine. I won't deny today sort of felt like he was, or like he could be one day, but whatever this is between Cara and Jack isn't something I can even think about right now.

She's on the brink of tears, talking so fast I can barely understand her. "Jack, please, oh thank God you're here! Can you head up to the rooftop for me? The new dining area is up there and tonight is the grand opening." She waves her hands around rapidly. "A water pipe broke and now there's water everywhere up there and I don't know what to do. Will you go up and just try to salvage something for me? I have to stay in the kitchen right now, but I'll make it up when I can!" With that she turns and practically runs back into the kitchen. Jack turns to look at me, wide eyed and with brows raised. He obviously has no idea what to do next either, but in true Jack Turner fashion, he jumps into action. He grabs my hand and walks briskly through the restaurant to the far corner where the elevator takes patrons up to the rooftop.

"What are we going to do?" I ask him as we enter the elevator.

Under his breath he says, "I have no idea." For some reason, I think I can sense some amusement in his voice. That doesn't make sense though, because Jack would never find someone else's misfortune amusing. The elevator doors open to a beautiful view of concrete covered in greenery and twinkle lights, with the sky and setting sun beyond. It looks like a fairy garden turned into a restaurant. There are tables set up far enough from each other that each party would feel like they had the roof to themselves. My eyes scan the entire place and notice that only one table is set.

"Jack?" I whisper while reaching for his hand behind me.

He replies softly, "Hmm?"

"There's no water up here."

"No, there's no water." His calloused fingers have enclosed mine and he's gently rubbing his thumb over the top of my hand. He's always soothing me. He's my calm in every storm.

I spin around quickly to catch the infamous dimple, because I heard it in his words, and now I want to see it. Like sunshine on a cloudy day, his smile is one of pure joy and satisfaction.

I'm sure I'm failing miserably, but I try to keep my face stern as I say, "What did you do?"

His smile turns sheepish, and he starts to shift on his feet. I was mostly kidding; I've figured out that he must have planned this dinner, but why is he so nervous right now?

"Jack?"

"I have a confession." He doesn't look up at first, but then he does and there's something in his eyes that I can't name, and I don't know if I've ever seen him look quite this vulnerable. "I planned all of this."

I let out the breath I'd been holding, with a little laugh. "I kinda put that together. I'm slow, but I'm not that slow."

"No, I mean I planned everything. This whole day. It was all a set up,

Sara." He winces as he gauges my reaction. It's sweet that he's this worried about how this might make me feel, but it's also crazy to me that he thinks I might be mad.

What have I done to this man?

He spent the whole day walking around town, playing games and buying Andi anything and everything. He bought cotton candy and caramel popcorn, then split them with her so she could have both without getting a tummy ache. He rode countless carnival rides, forced me to conquer my fear of the Ferris wheel, supported me going up against my parents downstairs, set up this incredibly romantic rooftop dinner, and it was all planned and calculated to a tee? If he thinks this would make me angry then I have been doing life so horribly wrong.

I want to wrap my arms around his neck and take away all the uncertainty that I see on his face. I want to tell him that I love it, that I loved the whole day and that he is turning out to be everything I thought I didn't need in my life. But something holds me back. I can't just jump into this–whatever this is–without thinking about the future first, about my heart, and most of all, Andi's heart. I know mine won't survive being broken again.

"Jack, you can breathe, I'm not mad." I laugh as he audibly releases his breath. He still seems so unsure, so I take his hand and hold it against my chest, over my heart. "I love it. I've loved this whole day, it's been amazing."

"Really? You're okay with this?" He waves his free hand to the beautiful set up behind me.

I look over my shoulder, at the breathtaking view of the sunsetting over our town, and softly say, "It's beautiful, Jack."

He turns his hand in mine and leads me to the table that someone has set up for two. There's a large covered pot filled with spaghetti and meatballs, garlic bread wrapped in tinfoil, and a couple beer bottles on ice. He thought of everything. He pulls my chair out for me and then gently slides it in behind me as I sit.

As he takes his seat across from me, I look down at my worn cut off jeans and black tank top. "I feel so underdressed for how fancy this is. Maybe some warning would have been better."

"You're perfect just the way you are, love."

Love. His voice is so tender and it really does something to my insides when he calls me that. The sun setting is reflected in his brown eyes. People say brown eyes are boring, that they're just brown. Not his, though. They're so light right now, compared to the deeper brown they often are. The way he's looking at me feels like he's using them to read my soul. My cheeks are flushed from his compliment. Why do they always do that? I feel like I'm just walking around with flaming cheeks anytime I'm in his presence. It's really kind of annoying. My annoyance vanishes when I see a piece of paper folded and sticking out from under my plate. What the heck? I slide it out and see my name written in Jack's messy writing on the front. I hold it up for him to see with one eyebrow raised.

"And what might this be?" I ask him with a grin.

His shy side is showing again as he says, "Just a note, I wrote it and gave it to Cara to put up here in case I needed something extra to smooth this whole thing over." He's smiling now, no doubt gloating on the inside that the note was unnecessary.

"Can I still read it?" I pretend to peek between the folds of paper.

"Of course." He smiles now, with all the confidence that I've always known Jack Turner to possess. It's sweet and endearing to see him a little insecure sometimes, but it's more comforting to see him like this. He's more predictable; he knows what he wants and he lays it all out on the table. There are no games or puzzles with Jack, and I love that. I don't think I gave that part of him enough credit all these years. I dismissed him so quickly, so lost in my own grief that I missed how easy this could have been. He's never been anything but open and honest about his intentions and feelings. Something about that was scary back then, but now it might just be exactly what I need.

I unfold the paper carefully and smile at the printing that is so, Jack. It's not a fancy script that you'd see in a Hallmark movie, it's not super neat teacher printing, it's just Jack's writing. I'm not even sure how I recognize it, to be honest. If there was any question who wrote this note, there wouldn't be as I read it, the words are so distinctly his.

Sara,

I've waited for seven years, maybe longer if I'm being honest with myself, but let's not do that tonight. I've waited for any opportunity to spend a day with you like we did today. I've waited to be able to show you how it could be between us, how I can make you happy. Not all the time, but most of the time. If you're pissed at me for hijacking your day, I just need you to know that it was so long in the making that when this opportunity presented itself, there was nothing that could've stopped me. Don't be mad at Noah or Liam or Cara. They're innocent, I promise. If you've kicked me off this rooftop, please enjoy your meal anyway, and think of me sobbing myself to sleep while you watch the fireworks. But to be sure, this isn't the last note you'll get from me. I'll still be waiting, for however long you need, to see that you are it for me.

Yours,

Jack

Well, holy shit. What am I supposed to do with that? Didn't I just say he doesn't play games and always tells it how it is.

I am it for him?

My reflexes are telling me to pack a doggy bag of spaghetti and run. But the look in Jack's eyes as he watches me, first reading his lovely words then contemplating my next move, cleaves a fissure in my heart. How many times have I broken this man? How many times have I turned away from him? And for what? What did it get me? It didn't stop us from losing Mark, it didn't stop this grief that I've carried around for seven long years from swallowing me whole some days. I've carried it for a long time, but make no mistake, *I have carried it!* I survived. I am here and I'm ready for it to feel like it. I want to live. Maybe I want to love. I don't know if it's that easy, to just flip that switch, but when I look at him, I know that I want to try.

I fold the paper the way it was when I found it and slip into my purse. I meet his eyes, refusing to be scared by these feelings tonight. I reach across the table and take his hand, "Thanks for waiting Jack."

As soon as we finish the last bites of our meal, the sky lights up with fireworks. I can't believe how perfect this evening has been. I feel like I've lived a day in someone else's life. In my life, there are no days like this. There is only work, stress, sadness and some shining happy moments with Andi weaved throughout. But this day... This day was everything. I stand and rest my hands against the rail that surrounds the rooftop. This night is turning out to be just as wonderful and I can't help but think, *if I'm dreaming, just let me sleep*.

"I'd miss the gorgeous, green spray in your eyes if I let you sleep."

Crap, did I say that out loud?

A deep rumble, almost like a laugh, comes from Jack's throat. "Yes, you said that out loud."

Okay, I know I did not say that out loud. I swat his chest gently. "You're making that hard to believe since you're reading my mind. Stop!"

He laughs harder and wraps his arm around my back and tucks me into his side. "I can read your facial expressions and body language. They were saying that you didn't mean to voice that thought, and then that you were surprised that you had. No mind reading, just 'Sara reading'. I've been reading you for years, love."

"When did you start seeing me?" I don't know for sure that I want the answer to that question but I feel like it's important for me to know.

"I don't honestly know. I've always respected you, I always knew you were loving and caring for everyone in the background. Amy was loud and in charge, but you were quietly her strength."

My breath hitches. What is he saying? She was my strength, that's why I fell apart when she died. I was nobody without her.

He turns so he can see my face. "Sara, did you not know that?"

I stutter over my words. "I think you're wrong, that's all." I tell him how it really was between us. Amy was the strong one. But he just shakes his head.

"You two held each other up. You don't think she'd fall apart if your roles were reversed? You were everything to her." He holds my face in his hands for the second time tonight and it almost brings me to my knees. "I don't know why she was taken from you, but I will never be sorry that you're here with me right now. Your strength is unprecedented. I think I saw that before Amy died. I saw you and everything that you are, but when Amy died and you kept standing, you proved everything I already knew. You do it again everyday with Andi."

He's left me speechless, but then again this man has a habit of doing that. He makes silence comfortable. There's never pressure to fill it, or pressure to do anything really. I can just be myself. Maybe for the first time since Amy died.

I lay my head on his chest where it so naturally wants to rest when he holds me like this and I whisper up to him, "I'm sorry that I hurt you."

He kisses my forehead and then tilts my chin up with his index finger so that I can't look anywhere but into his eyes. "You protected yourself. If that hurt me, so be it. All that matters is that you honoured yourself, your needs, your grief, and your heart. I won't lie to you and say it didn't hurt, but I will tell you that I understand. That's why I'm here, babe. I was waiting for you to be ready, because I knew it wasn't me you were fighting. It was you."

CHAPTER

Eleven

Sara

We cross town in Jack's truck, heading for my place, so lost in each other and conversation we forget to stop for my car. "I can work from home in the morning, it's fine," I say.

Jack furrows his brow. "Are you sure? I don't mind going back, it'll take five minutes."

"Nah, I'm tired." I squeeze his hand that's resting gently on my thigh. "And I don't want to get out of the truck right now anyway."

The look of genuine peace on his face makes me feel like I hung the moon. His hand on my leg and the other gripping the steering wheel is drawing my eye away from his gorgeous face. His forearm flexes as he turns the wheel and it does things to me. Shit, I thought that was a myth. It's definitely not.

Why did I fight this for so long?

He creeps to a stop in front of my house. It still sounds weird when talking about this house, but it finally feels like I'm making it home. I didn't give myself a chance to feel it before, but I feel closer to Amy when I'm here. I feel her just over my shoulder as I make breakfast for Andi, and I feel her watching Disney movies with us after dinner. I can hear her in my head telling me what I need to be focusing on with Andi and what isn't as important as I think it is. She's always telling me she's here with me and that I'm strong enough to do this. I tell her that I'm not, not without her, but she reminds me that she's not really gone, just her physical body is. Opening my mind and my heart to her home and to her daughter feels like it's opened me back up to her. I feel her in every fiber of my being again, and it's enough to make me think she might be right. Maybe I'm not alone and maybe I can do this.

Jack rounds the front of the truck and opens my door. Who said chivalry was dead? He reaches for my hand, and I let him take it. The feeling of his calloused fingers wrapped around mine is so natural it almost makes me ache with the familiarity. I want to savour the comfort and peace that I feel in this moment because if I know me, it will slip away as soon as he leaves tonight. We walk slowly, hand in hand to my front porch. Neither of us have much to say; it's as if we're both afraid to break the magic that has been the last twelve hours. When we reach the steps, he turns toward me and silently pulls me into his arms. I couldn't fight the fall against his chest even if I wanted to, and for once, I don't want to. I want to fall as hard and as fast as my heart will let me. I want this man wrapped around me; I want him to hold my face in his hands and whisper sweet words to me. I want to watch Andi climb on him for piggyback rides and then snuggle together on the couch for movie night. I want it all. I think he's been gently holding my heart for all these years; I just couldn't see it. I refused to let him in before, but just like he predicted, I am finally ready. And here he is, waiting patiently.

He whispers into my hair, "What are you thinking about, Sara?"

I smile against his chest. "I thought you could read me? Why don't you tell me?"

Looking up at him with a cheeky smile and a confidence I've never felt with anyone but him, I stretch up on my tiptoes to kiss his lips. When I lean back just a little to gauge his reaction, I see a heat in his eyes I have never seen before. I want more of that. I lean in again, but he meets me before I get there. His lips crash into mine with a passion I've only read about in romance novels. He kisses me like he's been waiting his whole life for this moment. Hell, maybe he has, but I want more. I want to be closer. I push myself up against him and everything that he is. My hands wrap around his neck and my fingers get lost in his dark hair. My heart feels like it's beating out of my chest. He's holding me so tight he must be able to feel it. I feel like I'm being swept away by a current, everything around me is slowly disappearing except the feel of his hard body against mine and the familiar smell of Old Spice mixed with pine that has never made my stomach flip quite like it is right now. Nothing else matters except this man and his mouth on mine—

"Hey! You know, if you need it, there's a room with a bed on the other side of that door, eh? Even the couch might be better than standing out here for your neighbours to see."

Noah.

Shit.

Hysterical laughter and knee slapping from the porch next door follows my brother's rude interruption of the best kiss of my life. Even though my cheeks are flaming in embarrassment, and I can't help but cover my face with my hands, Jack is trying his best not to burst out laughing. The heat I saw in his eyes a moment ago has turned to mirth. Ugh, boys.

I yell across the yard to the idiot still laughing like a fool on his front porch. "Seriously, Noah? Must you?"

"Yes, I must." He's wiping tears from his eyes, for God's sake. What a loser.

"Have you been sitting there the whole time? You little creeper." If I'm honest I didn't even notice his truck parked in front of his house when we pulled in, but I think it's safe to say I was a little distracted.

"Yup. I definitely have; thanks for not giving me more of a show. I appreciate that. It looked like it was starting to escalate so I thought I'd save myself."

I wish I had something to throw at him, but I don't, and Jack is full-on laughing now so what am I going to do? I swat his chest in mock annoyance. "Okay, you're as bad as him, stop!"

"What? You have to admit it's pretty funny. The poor guy almost got more than he bargained for, living next door to his little sister."

"Oh my gosh, you two. That's it, I'm going inside." I glare over to where Noah is still sitting on his porch even though he likely can't see me and yell, "Alone!"

Jack leans towards me to whisper in my ear. His breath on my neck sends goosebumps over my bare arms. "I don't care that he's watching, I'm not leaving here without kissing you goodnight."

"What was that just now, if not a goodnight kiss?"

He smiles wide, dimple and all. "Oh babe, that was just a taste of what is to come." With that he rests his lips gently on the spot where my neck meets my shoulder, then again on the edge of my jaw. Slowly, almost painfully slow, he makes his way to the corner of my mouth, then finally, his lips press gently against mine. Only for a second, but it's enough to ignite my core right back to where it was before my idiotic brother interrupted. Speaking of that idiot, he calls across the yard again, "Still here!"

Our smiles break the kiss and Jack walks backwards down the drive towards where his truck is parked. "I'll call you tomorrow. Don't slam this door, Sara. This is it, we made it." Within seconds he's behind the wheel and driving away.

I turn away from where Jack's truck just vanished down the driveway that heads to the main road and see Noah crossing his lawn to mine. I smile shyly at him. "All jokes aside, I'm sorry you had to see that."

He barks out a laugh. "Sara, all jokes aside, I'm sorry it took you so damn long to give that guy a chance on your porch."

Did I just hear him right? He's fine with everything he just saw; more than fine, he seems happy. I pick my jaw up off the ground and ask him to clarify. "What do you mean by that?"

In an exasperated voice, like I'm a toddler who can't remember three comes after two, he says, "Come on! It's been years, he's been pining, waiting, hoping, showing up, then walking away, but pining this whole time! It's been painful to watch. You can be a real bitch, you know?"

Affronted, I scoff, "I am not!" Even though I just had those same thoughts earlier tonight, I won't admit that to him.

He laughs and runs his hand through his sandy-coloured hair. It's always matched mine. His eyes have the green through the hazel like mine too. I'm struck by the familiarity of him and of this, standing in our yards chatting about life. It's how it would have been for Amy and me, and I'm sure he did this same thing countless nights with Mark. Now we have each other, and I think it's time I acknowledge and embrace that. I get to live next door to my brother and raise my niece for my sister on the same farm that we grew up on. What a blessing that is amidst this heartache and grief.

"Noah, I'm sorry if I haven't been here for you these last six months. I can't even begin to imagine what it must feel like for you to go to work every day and not have Mark there with you and then on top of that you have to come home and he's not here either. I've been a little lost and I feel like I've failed you because I was too worried about myself."

"Sar, you're crazy. It's been rough, yeah, but you aren't failing anybody. I love you, we all do, and we just want to help you with everything you're wading through. I know, just like with Amy, we all lost Mark, but it's different for you, again. With Amy you lost your best friend and only sister and now you've lost Mark, but also been tasked with raising Andi. It's a lot–I don't envy you–but don't for a second think you have to do it alone. That guy right there," he points down the driveway to where Jack just disappeared, "He will be here to help you through anything that could ever come your way. You have me, Liam and Jenna, and Mom and Dad. No matter how overbearing they can be, they want to help too, but sometimes they just don't know how."

Tears fill my eyes. "I know. I do know that. I just have such a hard time loosening my grip on control. When everything feels so out of control, if I can just deal with all this stuff on my own, I feel like I've accomplished something. I know it's dumb, and to be honest, I'm tired. I'm so tired of carrying it alone."

He wraps me in his strong arms and rubs my back like he used to when I was little after falling off the swing that hung from the tree in Mom and Dad's yard.

"I'm sorry you didn't see it before, but I'm glad you're there now. Grief is too heavy to carry alone. We aren't made to withstand it that way. We might think it's better at the time but it's so much lighter if you share it with those around you."

"It feels like the better option because it hurts so much to think of relying on you guys to get through this and then losing you too."

"Sara! You're not going to lose us; we aren't going anywhere."

"Like Amy wasn't going anywhere? And Mark, you don't think he planned to walk Andi down the aisle at her wedding? Of course he did." I can't help the bitter tone of my voice; it's become second nature unfortunately.

Noah shakes his head. "Sara, you can't focus on that shit. You can't stay holed up in this house alone for the rest of your life, working your shitty job that you hate, just to prevent losing someone you love. Would you go back and change your relationship with Amy if you knew you were going to lose her? Would you keep her at a distance and never love her like you did?"

"No. Of course not!" *It's not the same thing though*, I think to myself.

Another mind reader here, because he says, "It's exactly the same thing. You're trying to stop yourself from needing and loving people around you, because why? You're afraid they might die? Sara, I don't mean to be a jackass, but do you know how stupid that is?"

"Well, it sounds pretty stupid when you say it like that. But God, Noah, I'm just so scared. It makes me want to throw up to think of what it would do to me if something happened to you or Liam. Or Jenna and Andi, and now Jack. After one day with him, I want to protect him from any danger or disease that might take him from me. I know it's dumb, but I can't help it and it's crippling sometimes."

His tone softens. "I'm sorry I said it was stupid, because it's not. It's a real fear, I get that. I just want to help you get out from under it. Have you tried talking to a therapist? You've had so much piled on you. The fire department provided one for me and I can't tell you how much it's helped. I wish I had taken this step after Amy, but it's better late than never. I thought talking about it would be pointless. I can do that with Liam and Jack when I need to, but this is different. Someone removed and professional, to help you gain insight into why you think and feel the way you do and how you can cope with it all in a healthy way. It's really crazy but also amazing." He pauses for a second. "But to backtrack a little, do you think, if something happened to Jack before today, you wouldn't have been affected by it?"

I roll my eyes at him. "Okay, okay, I know what you're getting at, of course I would be."

"You two have been circling each other for years, but you know what would happen if something happened to him? You would feel the most intense guilt and regret. You would realize, too late, that you missed an opportunity to love an amazing human and to have him love you back. Jack doesn't do anything halfway. He will love you until the day he dies, through any hardship and trial. He is everything I could ever want in a partner for my sister. If I could choose anyone to be with you and raise Andi with you, it would be him. We all just got lucky in this case because he chose you too a long time ago. So, stop screwing around and figure your shit out."

I can't help but laugh at his intensity. Noah is never like this. "Holy, how long have you been holding all that in?"

"A really long fucking time." He laughs and shoves my shoulder.

"Thanks for everything, big brother. I love you, you know? And I love living next door to you, even if you did interrupt the best kiss of my life."

"Okay, okay, I love the guy, but I don't need any more details than that." He turns to walk back to his place but before he leaves, he looks at me seriously. "You okay? Are you going to give Jack a chance?"

I sigh. "Yes, I can see he deserves a lot more from me than what I've given him. Thanks for today by the way, I know you were in on his little plan." He winks at me with pride in their conspiring, "But I don't know how quickly I can just change my entire way of thinking; self-preservation runs deep."

Noah huffs a laugh and makes his way to his porch and heads inside. Before his door shuts behind him, he calls out to me, "I love you, sister."

I smile, "I love you, brother."

Feeling exhausted and overwhelmed by this influx of emotions and realizations, I slowly make my way to my bed. As I lay on my back, staring at the ceiling and trying to figure out what I'm going to do with my life, my phone buzzes on the table beside me.

Jack- *Don't overthink it, babe. I'm not going anywhere, and we have all the time in the world to figure this out.*

Mind reader.

Sara- *Get out of my head. And I know, you've been telling me that for years. I'm just catching up, okay?*

Jack- *Glad to hear it. Goodnight, beautiful.*

My cheeks warm at the compliment and he's not even here. I'm such a goner.

Sara- *Thanks for waiting, Jack.*

I'm so happy he waited for me. I slide my phone back on the table and close my eyes, trying to settle my mind. I let my thoughts wander to what it would be like to let my guard down, to let Jack in for real. We could have so many days just like today. We could be truly happy. That's something I didn't think I would ever be again, but he makes me feel like it's possible.

CHAPTER Twelve

Sara

"Sara, I need all the tea. What is going on with Jack? I know there was something, by the way. I've been biding my time, but my patience is wearing thin."

I just sat down across from Jenna at her favourite table at Liam's. It's the furthest from the crowds that are sometimes packed in here, tucked away in the back corner. I guess if I have to 'spill the tea', as she put it, I could at least do it back here where no one else will hear.

I sigh heavily and wrap my hands around my hot mug of coffee. "I wish I knew what was going on, to be honest. I am such a mess; I don't know what to do."

"What do you mean? Was Saturday amazing? Sorry for bailing, but the guys had this awesome plan and I just loved it so much that I had to let it play out. Was it okay? You weren't mad, were you?"

"No, no, I wasn't mad, it was amazing. But it's Tuesday now and I feel like a fish out of water. We've texted but I just don't know what's next. Why do I feel like a schoolgirl?" I sigh and roll my eyes, "Also, I still can't believe Noah and Liam were a part of that, but I had the best day. Honestly, it was almost too good to be true. I think that's what's scaring me."

Jenna looks at me with compassion but also sadness in her eyes. "Oh

Sara, love is scary. You're preaching to the choir here. Did I not just run away from everything that was scaring the crap out of me, for the second time?"

"It's not the same. You embraced Liam so fast and found your place, then life punched us all in the face, again. And now you're getting married, you've moved in with him, you guys are doing so amazing. I don't know how to get out of my own way. How did you swallow the grief and move toward Liam instead of away from him?"

"First of all, he didn't give me a choice. He knows my heart better than I do. Secondly, the grief is still there, every single day. I wake up with tears in my eyes, reliving the night we lost Mark. You know it doesn't go away. I know you still feel that way about Amy and it's been seven years."

"It's true, not tears every single day but always something. A thought, a memory, sometimes a cry, or a laugh, she's still a part of everything. I had a good chat with Noah on Saturday night and he reminded me that I would never trade my time and love that I had with Amy, for this grief. The same goes for Mark, and for anyone we could lose any second of any day."

"Talk to Jack about it. Tell him you're scared; not of him, but of losing him. He'll understand and work through it with you. You deserve love and happiness, Sar; today is the day you start taking care of yourself and not so much everyone else." She grabs my hand and drags me from my seat, towards the door.

"Whoa! Wait. Where are we going?"

"We're going to the Balsam News to give Jerry your resignation."

I yank my hand from hers and stop walking immediately. "What? Jenna, what are you talking about? I can't quit my job. What does that have to do with anything anyway?"

"You're miserable working there. I don't know if you always have been, but you have been since I came home last year. I hate seeing you this way. Something has to change, and you seem to work better when you don't have a choice." She smiles and lifts her one shoulder as if to say, 'whatchya gonna do'. Brat.

"Jenna, come back and sit down. You're crazy." I don't give her a chance to answer before I go back to our table and take my seat again.

She throws herself down into her chair and says, "Tell me one reason you shouldn't quit your job today."

"Easy, I need a paycheck."

"Nope. I know you don't. Mark left you enough to care for Andi and yourself, without having to work."

My eyes widened at her knowledge of that, but I shouldn't be surprised. Mark was her best friend, he would've told his sister everything he had set up, should anything happen to him. I've often wondered why Jenna wasn't the one he chose to take care of Andi but was always too afraid to ask. I don't know if she holds any resentment toward me for that, but since she's kind of brought it all up, maybe now is the time.

"Jen, do you know why Mark asked me to care for Andi and not you?" I keep my eyes down, examining the coffee in my mug.

She reaches her hand across the table and places it on top of mine. I lift my eyes to see her gentle smile. "Amy wanted you to raise her daughter if Mark couldn't. She was always very clear about that, and he would never take that from her, even if she'd never know. You're a caretaker, Sara. She's your sister's girl, she belongs with you. I worried that you would think I would be offended and that it would drive a wedge between us. Please know that I could never be. I love you both so much. I will always be here to support you and Andi in anything you need, but I will never second guess a choice that two parents' have made for their child."

I find myself smiling back as I squeeze her hand. "Thanks, Jenna. That means so much to me. And since you probably know more than I do about Mark's finances, you know I don't have to work but—"

"I know Mark didn't want you to have to work, but I also know that he wanted you to be happy. If writing for the paper made you happy, he wouldn't bat an eye. Neither would I, but it's so painfully obvious that it's burning you out, especially with everything that comes along with raising Andi. I'm happy to help with her whenever you need, but I think what you really need is to put your own wants and needs in the forefront and you'll find it inadvertently benefits that little girl. She needs you at your best; happiness and health are key."

"Okay, I hear you, but I don't know, Jen. It just feels like taking advantage of Mark's money, and his death. It feels icky."

"I kinda get that, but it's just not true. This is what he wanted, for you and for his daughter. You can't deny that he and Amy would want you to do whatever you need to, to give Andi the best life you can."

"No, I won't deny that."

"Okay, now only you can decide what that looks like. You're my best friend, Sara. I can tell you what I see, and what I think I know, but only you can say what will make you happy. That's why I didn't push you about Jack last Christmas when I wanted to and that's why I didn't stop the boys on Saturday when they planned to ambush you with the date of the century." We both laugh then, thinking about the three burly farm boys planning and scheming a fancy date day. So hilarious.

"Thanks, Jenna, I needed this chat." I lift my coffee to my lips and say, "And this coffee." My sip of coffee reminds me that it's never as good as when Sherri was the one who made it. "When is Sherri planning to come back to town? Is she still planning to?"

Jenna sets her mug down on the table and contemplates for a second. "Yeah, I think she will. She's in a weird place. I think she's just struggling, comparing her grief to ours. That never works, we know that. But she's just trying to figure out where she fits here now. She was only with Mark for a short time, but it meant a lot to her, and she can't just go back to the way it was before. None of us can. I'm hopeful she'll figure out what she needs and go after it. If we're lucky it'll lead her back here."

I have an hour before I need to get Andi from school, so I text Jack.

Sara- *Hey, are you around? Okay if I pop by your place before I get Andi?*

I see the three little dots pop up right away and smile as I wait for his response.

Jack- *I'm here. I'll meet you at the house. In five?*

Sara- *Yup, see you soon.*

I'm smiling ear to ear as I drive across town to Jack's farm. He must love that it's so far out of town, away from the bustle of the townspeople. Our family farm is just down the first road east of town but his place is as far north as you can go and still call it Balsam River, which isn't very far. No stop lights still make it just a five-minute drive from the middle of town where Liam's Coffee and Books is.

Just thinking about him makes me feel so giddy. I don't know how I fought this happiness off for seven years but I'm so ready to let my heart feel. As I pull in his drive and see him leaning against the post on his porch my stomach does a tumble. He's waiting for me. He's been waiting for so long. I take my fill before I get out of my Jeep, I could get used to finally being able to stare at him unabashedly. No shame fills my chest or my cheeks as I remember his hands holding my face when he kissed me for the first time.

As I climb out, he gives me a little wave and makes his way over to me.

"Hey." I didn't mean for it to come out as a whisper, but it does anyways.

His lips slowly curve up into his signature smile. "Hey."

This is the first time I've seen him since Saturday, but we've been texting nonstop the last two days, so this shouldn't be weird. I can feel the old habit of making it that way trying to come to the surface. I can be awkward as hell, and that's why most people think I'm a bitch if they don't know me well. Jack was never fooled. He's always known me better than

I gave him credit for. I can be myself with him, my true self. I am loving and kind and I deserve to be loved. I will not hide from that anymore.

He's standing in front of me when I turn from closing my door. I tilt my head slightly to look up into his eyes, they're chocolate brown today. Before I can change my mind, I wrap my arms around his waist and lean into his chest. His arms are instantly around me and holding me tightly. I lift my head slightly and place a kiss on the side of his neck and rest my head against his shoulder.

He speaks low against my hair, "Hey, you okay?"

He can't see but I smile. "I am now."

He holds me tighter and we just stand there for what could be minutes or hours. I get lost in his arms, his fingers playing with the long strands of my hair. When I finally remember why I wanted to come here, I lift my head and pull back just enough to see his face. I place a gentle kiss on his lips and his smile instantly spreads across his whole face. That dimple is out in full force, and his eyes are shining so brightly. I did that. I love seeing the effect I have on him.

"I never thought there'd come a day when I would get to hold you like this, and you'd look up at me and kiss me like that. You're making all my dreams come true, love. And it's only Tuesday."

I can't help but laugh. Not at him, but at how amazingly wonderful this is. How easy it is to be loved by him. "I'm sorry I made you doubt us. I'm sorry I made you wait so long."

"Don't be sorry, I'd wait a thousand lifetimes even if all I ever got was this moment right here, right now, with you in my arms."

Swoon. What did I do to deserve this man? "Have I thanked you for that lately?"

He laughs. "Yeah, a couple times I think."

I reach up and kiss him again. "Thanks for waiting, Jack."

I press both my hands to his chest, not wanting to leave his arms but to instead talk to him about everything Jenna said. He has so quickly become the person I want to talk these things out with and the person whose opinion means the most to me.

"I just wanted to talk to you about something, and I had some time before I had to pick up Andi from school. Do you have time?"

His brow furrows. "Sure, of course, but you seem like something's wrong, even though you said you're okay now."

"I am, it's just some things Jenna said while we had coffee and lunch earlier. I don't know how I feel about them, and I thought if I could talk it out with you maybe things would become a little clearer."

He gently rubs my arms with his hands and says softly, "Of course, Sar, what was she saying?"

I relay my conversation with Jenna to him and fill in the gaps of Amy and Mark's wishes too. I know Amy always planned to be a stay-at-home mom. Not that she would have ever expected me to do that, but Jenna's not wrong that they would want me to be happy in whatever way I chose to raise Andi.

"I've always wanted to write a novel. Jenna knows that from last winter when she opened her flower shop. We had a great night one night talking about all our dreams and how we'd make them come true. I didn't think it would ever be possible for me. I was always too drained from running the paper to give it any attention and I couldn't have afforded my Jeep and apartment if I quit my job and spent my days writing something that may never make a dime. After Mark it's been even crazier; emotionally and physically exhausting just making it through each day and trying to find my groove. I just don't know if it's really what is best for Andi."

"I trust one hundred percent that whatever you do, you will make sure it works out in Andi's favour, but I agree with you that it can't be about you getting to live your dream, by finally being able to write a book. As cool as that would be–and I know you would rock it out of this world–you're right to think of Andi first. Maybe take some time to really evaluate your days and energy and how much you're giving to the newspaper and how much you have left for yourself and Andi. I will be honest, I didn't know you were unhappy at the paper until you let it slip awhile ago, but I agree with Jenna that it's crucial to Andi's well-being that your mental health is in a good place. We don't always have control over our emotions, our hormones, our families, or our jobs, but you have the chance to take control of your job. You have options, and yes, that is thanks to Mark, but that doesn't make it less than, just because he's not here and he's left you this gift of freedom. He would want you to use it, whatever that might look like for you."

I want to cry and laugh and hug and kiss him all at the same time. I want to tell him that I love him, but that feels a little premature. Leave it to me, zero to sixty, over here in the fast lane.

Instead, I smile at him in wonder and say, "How do you always know just what to say?"

He huffs out a laugh. "I don't, trust me. But I've been Kristin's sounding board for our entire lives, so I've learned to be a good listener, and I know you. I know you need to look at all the angles before you make a decision. You're obviously not going to go into town and quit your job today, but Jenna's not wrong that it is something to think about."

"Thank you. Thank you for listening and sharing your honest opinion, but also for believing in me. Even when I don't always believe in myself, you're still there with support. I can't even believe how much I took you for granted all these years. Never again, Jack, never again."

He stands from where we found seats on his porch step and takes my hand. He pulls me gently into his arms for another award-winning hug. Who knew that was a thing?

"Did you know you could solve the problems of the world with your hugs?"

"Did you accidentally voice your inside thoughts again?"

I laugh,."Ha, no. I really was wondering if you knew. They're powerful things these arms you have here." I squeeze his bicep hard and flinch when it has zero give. "My God, Jack, how often do you work out?"

He laughs harder now. "I don't really, it's just from working on the farm. I use my arms more than anything, planting trees, pruning them, and even cutting them down, then hauling them all onto the wagon to get them back here to sell. Farming of any kind is a workout on its own."

I flash him a cheeky grin. "Well, I'm here for it now, I hope you're ready to be ogled."

"By you? I've been ready for years."

I let out a loud squeal as he lifts my feet off the ground and swings me around in his arms. My long hair is blowing in the wind and tangles around my face and makes its way into his mouth. He laughs while spitting it out. "That went much smoother in my head."

I can't control my laughter as he sets me down and I try to clear my thick waves from my face. "With this much hair, nothing ever goes as planned."

He laughs again and swats my ass gently as I open the door to my Jeep. "Can I bring dinner over later for us and Andi?"

I don't even hesitate before I say, "Sure, is six okay?"

"Perfect, see you then!"

As I drive back across town to our farm, I push aside any intruding thoughts about this being too good to be true. Maybe it isn't. Maybe this is life, the good and bad, grief and joy. Like Mark always said, find the joy and let it live beside your grief. I think I'm finally figuring out how to do that.

CHAPTER *Thirteen*

Jack

To say the last month with Sara and Andi have been amazing would be an understatement. I can't even remember how I lived my life without these two beautiful girls at the center of it. Andi is smiling down at me from atop her horse, Daisy, waiting for me to pass her the reins. I've spent the last few weeks bringing her over to her lessons for Sara and hanging out with her back at their house afterwards. I have the time, it's quiet around my place until fall, and Sara wanted to try to get Andi spending more time at home and not so much being carted from relative to relative. As much as they all love spending the time with the baby of their family and want to help Sara in any way they can, it's not ideal that Andi wasn't getting to be at home very much while Sara was working. This way, I get my much-loved time with this little girl, and she gets to be at home as often as possible. Except when she's riding of course; in all honesty I think she'd live in the barn if we let her.

"Uncle Jack, come on! I'm ready to go!" Andi prods my arm with the toe of her boot. I pass her the reins and she trots over to the round pen where Charlie is waiting. He's a high school kid trying to earn some extra cash to get his own horse. He's ridden horses here with Brent for as long as I can remember. He helps out pretty often, and he's great with Andi. You can tell he doesn't have much experience with kids, but he knows horses. When he's the only one with the time to help her figure out this riding thing we make a pretty good team. I have zero experience with horses but I'm an expert on Andi Ryan, so together we make it through these afternoons with lots of laughs and smiles. Noah spends a lot of afternoons out here with him, riding or fixing fences. They both pick up a lot of the work that Brent doesn't have time for anymore. Noah mentioned that he wants to have him join us out at my place sometime soon. It turns out he doesn't have a lot to go home to. There's a lot of talk around town about his family; they say he's been fending for himself for a few years and I'm pretty sure he's only fifteen. I try to listen to talk, but I'm glad Noah takes the time to hang out with him when he can. Brent has taught him all there is to know about ranch work and says he's a damn hard worker. He'll be alright if he sticks around the Ryans.

"Hey, Uncle Jack, why don't you ride horses?"

I stutter a little over my answer. I'm not in the habit of admitting to this girl that I couldn't touch the moon if she asked me to. "I... umm... well, I just never have, peanut."

She tilts her head sideways, looking at me with a very confused look on her face. "But you and Uncle Noah have been friends for a long time and Uncle Liam too, and you were my daddy's friend. They all ride horses."

I laugh at how her mind works. She can't imagine someone not riding horses every chance they get. "I wasn't good friends with your uncles and daddy until we were older, and they didn't ride much by then. I know they did it for work with your grandpa, but it just wasn't something they ever asked me to do with them for fun." I shrug my shoulders. "It's okay though, horses aren't really my thing. I like living things that are planted in the ground and don't move until I chop them down."

She bursts out laughing. God, I love that sound. It's like rain sprinkling on a summer day. "You're so funny, Uncle Jack. Why don't you ask Charlie to teach you—" She squeals and claps her hands, "Oh! Oh! Uncle Jack, will you ride with me and Charlie? He can teach us both! Oh please! That would be so fun!"

Would it though? What have I gotten myself into? I wasn't ever planning on putting my ass in a saddle, I just wanted to spend some time with Andi while she does what she loves. It was a bonus that it would help Sara out at the same time.

Shit!

I rub my jaw with my hand. "Ah… I don't know, peanut, that's a big move. I've never been on a horse in my life. I don't know if Charlie's qualified to teach an old man like me."

Charlie leans over the rail of the round pen. "That's alright, Mr. Turner, I taught my uncle to ride last year. He's a little older than you, but same thing, never been in the saddle and was scared shi– I mean, crapless, poopless? I don't know, he was really scared."

"It's Jack, and I'm not scared. I just don't know what the point is. I don't own a horse, or a farm that needs them. I'm happy to just watch Andi take her lessons."

He chuckles, and I'm not a fan of his tone when he says, "Well, *Jack*, Andi is almost ready for some short trail rides on Daisy, and I bet she'd love to go with you rather than me. It's a great hobby and a great way to spend time with Andi and her Auntie Sara." He winks. The little jerk actually winks at me. If he wasn't a fifteen-year-old kid, I'd knock him upside the head. If Andi wasn't here I probably would anyway. He's really put me between a rock and a hard place, and by the stupid grin on his face he knows it.

"Yeah!" Andi yells excitedly. "I can't wait to trail ride! Uncle Liam and Auntie Jenna go on rides all the time. They're getting married so maybe if you and Auntie Sara can trail ride you could get married too!"

That has me choking and laughing at the same time. What I wouldn't give for it to be that simple. "Andi… peanut, riding horses has nothing to do with being in love or getting married."

"You don't love Auntie Sara?"

Double shit! How do I get out of this now? How did this riding lesson turn into the snake pit of twenty questions? I can not tell the seven-year-old that I'm in love with her aunt before I tell her aunt. Or can I?

"You know, Andi, I do love Auntie Sara, but I don't think she knows that yet. I've never told her, because I don't know if she loves me the same way," I add quickly, "And that's okay! She doesn't have to, because that's not why I love her. I think she will love me one day; she just has a lot of catching up to do."

Her smile splits across her face and makes her eyes crinkle like I just shone the sun right on her face. She giggles and says, "Oh Uncle Jack, you're so funny. She definitely loves you the same as Auntie Jenna loves Uncle Liam. She looks the exact same, she gets weird googly eyes, and she smiles and laughs so much when you come over. It's my favourite time when we all get to do things together because of that."

My heart is melting and it's not from this ridiculously hot June we're having. It's the words this little girl just shot right through my soul. I can only pray that she's right about how Sara feels, but I'm not taking any chances. "Does Auntie Sara like going on trail rides, peanut?" I give Charlie the side eye, mentally willing him to keep his mouth shut. I don't need a teenager gloating that he's giving me advice on how to woo a woman.

Andi looks to the barn for a minute, then back to me. She shrugs her one shoulder and says, "I don't know. She has a horse, but I've never seen her ride him. I think it would be fun for us to all trail ride together! Can we please? Will you learn? Please, Uncle Jack!"

I still don't know how anyone can tell this girl no. I'm about to get on a thousand-pound animal that I have zero skill in controlling and hope for the best, just because she asked me to. I want to say fuck my life, but the smile she's beaming down at me from Daisy's back is enough to make my life. She knows I would do anything for her and there's nothing else in this world I want more than her faith and trust.

Charlie left us in the pen. He asked me to supervise Andi walking around on her horse. I don't know the first thing about any of this but that's basic enough I guess. He went to find me a horse, but unfortunately he returned with Liam and Brent in tow.

He looks at me sheepishly. "I'm sorry, man, they wondered why I needed another horse. I needed a really quiet one for you and they were suspicious. I can't lie to save my life and Mr. Ryan is my boss! What was I supposed to do?"

I mumble under my breath, "For fuck's sake," low enough that Andi can't hear. I look past Charlie to where Liam and Brent are standing, both leaning on the hitching posts for tying horses up outside the round pen with shit-eating grins on their faces.

"Hop on, Jack, we're just here for moral support!" Liam calls out to me.

With nothing else left to do but get on the damn horse Charlie is holding in front of me, I lift my foot up and into the stirrup and swing my other one across the back to fall on the other side of the horse. My ass smacks down in the saddle in a highly uncomfortable manner. Liam barks a laugh at the wince he can clearly see on my face. I find my toes in the other stirrup quickly, trying not to show my nerves. Why am I doing this to myself? Oh right, the sweet little girl riding around in front of me. How is she keeping her butt in the saddle while she rides? She doesn't look any different than if she was sitting in a chair.

I glare down to where Charlie is standing. "Now what? I'm on, so far so good. Make this easy, kid."

He laughs, again. Damn kid, "Just hold your reins up like Andi is, front and center will tell him to go forward. When you need to stop, pull back and say, 'whoa'. His name is Burt and he likes it when you scratch his neck, so when he does a good job, do that. When you're ready to move, tap your heels lightly on his side and he'll go. He's super quiet, so he won't take off on you. Nothing to be scared of Mr. Turner."

"Charlie, I'm not scared. Are you gonna talk to me like I'm seven and then call me Mr. Turner? It's Jack."

I kick my heels like he said, and *Burt*, doesn't move. Well fuck. *Burt*, what kind of name is that for a horse anyways? "Liam, did you name this guy? Burt? What were you thinking? He hates you for it and is taking it out on me!"

Liam laughs and Brent answers, "I named him Jack, after my father."

Wow, the hits just keep on coming.

"Ah shit, I'm sorry, Brent, it's a great name. I'm sure he'll live up to his legacy. Can you just tell him to get moving so I can stop making an ass of myself up here?"

They're both killing themselves laughing now, completely useless to me.

"Uncle Jack, just do this." Andi puts her hand out forward with her reins, kicks the sides of Daisy pretty good, and makes a kiss noise with her mouth. Daisy trots forward in a circle as Andi guides her with her reins. Looks easy enough. I do just as she did, and Burt doesn't move.

"Brent, your horse is broken."

"Nah, he's just learning you as a rider first. He knows you're chicken shit and doesn't want to scare you by taking a step."

Called out even by a horse, great day for me today.

I take a deep breath. I watch Andi for a minute, and think of Sara and how cool it will be to ride with her one day, the three of us trail riding like Andi said. Even if Sara doesn't want to get back into riding, I think of all the memories I can make with Andi out here riding the trails of the Ryan farm. It's something she will miss getting to do with Mark as she grows up and I've made it my mission to be her second best. Alright, one last shot. I follow Charlie and Andi's instructions again. I swear I didn't do a single thing differently, but Burt takes a step, and then another. We're walking around the pen. He's following Daisy like it's his job. I know, man, I feel your pain too. Just follow her and you'll be good. I looked up to see Andi turned around in her saddle watching me, pride beaming from her eyes. "You did it! Good job, Uncle Jack!"

Liam and Brent actually have a similar look on their faces, then Liam says, "Way to go, man. Old dog, new tricks. It can be done."

"Screw you, I'm only two years older than you."

"Yeah exactly, there's no way I'd get on a horse for the first time at my age."

What an ass.

Brent interrupts Liam's laughter with a kind smile. "Good for you, Jack. The smile on Andi's face right now is worth every sore muscle you're going to have tomorrow."

"Wait, what? Sore muscles?"

Liam is laughing so hard he's crying and Brent just chuckles, shaking his head as they both walk back to the barn that they were working in before. I look over to see Charlie standing in the middle of the pen. "They're exaggerating right? How bad can it be?"

Charlie just looks down at the sand he's kicking around with the toe of his boot. "I'm sorry, man."

Well, shit. I think that's triple shit by now.

CHAPTER

Fourteen

Sara

"Hey Sar!" I hear Noah calling me from the barn furthest from where I'm standing. It's where they keep all the mares and new babies. They've had to be kept in during the days because they're so young and it is so stinkin' hot out here.

In some places in the world, at the end of June, this weather might be normal. But there's been years we still had snow in May up here, so this is just crazy! It's going to be a hard summer for farmers all around here if we don't get some rain. There's been fire bans put in place across the province for the last few weeks already. I'm sweating and wandering the farm looking for where Andi and my dad have gotten to. I checked in with Mom at the house and she said they were checking water troughs about a half hour ago. It would've been nice to find Andi in the house so I could use her as a buffer to not have to discuss my career with my mother. Liam has talked to her about the idea of me quitting my job to focus on writing a novel, and of course she isn't on board. She won't say that outright, but her subtle hints let me know that she would feel better if I had a consistent income. I don't disagree, I'm just trying to be open minded about it all because I truly believe that Jenna was right about what Amy and Mark would want, for me and for Andi too.

I yell back to Noah with a wave and then head in his direction. I was hoping I wouldn't run into any other family members until I got my hands on Andi but maybe he'll know where they've gotten to.

"How's it going? Have you seen Dad and Andi anywhere?"

"Oh yeah, they'll be back down this way shortly. They were just making sure all the yearlings had enough water. I've been trying to help out around here a little more with this weather, it makes a lot of extra work for dad."

"For sure, I'm happy you're around to help him. I feel bad when they have Andi here so much too. Just one more thing for them."

Noah shakes his head. "Nah, you're nuts, they love having her. She doesn't even slow him down. She just makes the regular jobs more fun."

I smile thinking of the relationship my parents have gotten to build with Andi these last couple of years. It really is good for all of them.

Noah takes his ball cap off and rakes his fingers through his sweaty hair. Yuck, I don't get why all the women in town drool over this sweaty man-child. Whether it's coming from work at the fire station, the basketball court with the guys, or working on the farm he's somehow always dirty and gross.

"So..." he hesitates to continue. Noah's nervous, which is weird, and he's still running his hands through his hair. "Liam mentioned Jenna talked to you about moving on from the paper and focusing on writing your own stuff."

I sigh and mumble under my breath, "Here we go."

Unfortunately, he hears me. "Hey now, what's that about? I didn't think it was a secret, he just wanted me to know what's been going on with you. We live next door to each other, Sar, I'd hope I don't have to get updates from Liam anymore, but here we are!"

"Listen, don't get mad, I just feel like I have so much going on, and so much to think about that I can't worry about keeping you all apprised of my thought processes, and honestly why should I? I know this is the first you've brought it up, but I'm so sick of Liam and Mom and Dad harping on me about it. They don't even share the same opinion but I'm still sick of it. I'll do what I think is best, when I think it's best, and that's all any of you need to know. Seriously, my God!"

He backs into the barn with both hands raised in front of his chest, like that'll protect him. "Whoa, okay sis, calm down. I honestly was just checking in. I wanted to know how you were doing, if you're handling everything alright, if there's anything I can do to help. I'm not here to throw my opinion at you."

I sigh in exasperation. Maybe I shouldn't have gone off on him like that, but I've had it with this family of mine thinking they need to be in the middle of everything. This is why I insisted on moving off the farm as soon as I was working full time. I could control the doses of Ryans and take as needed. "I'm sorry, Noah, that makes you the only one, so I wasn't expecting that."

"Don't let them get to you. You have killer instincts and your heart beats for that little girl. Don't let anyone tell you any different. You'll both be just fine no matter what choice you make. If you trip and fall, we'll be here to help you up, and there's no shame in that."

"You sound like Jack. I shouldn't have said you're the only one without opinions. He's been great too, just listens and supports me in every way. A little too good to be true, eh?"

"Nah, he's just sitting back watching you work the miracles you always work. He knows you've got this. Just don't be afraid to lean on him once in a while, or any of us for that matter."

I laugh lightly. "I know, I know. I'm just trying to keep my head above water. I'm working on grabbing the life preserver at the same time."

Noah wraps his arm around my shoulder, and I swear he reaches in and touches the corners of my heart when he says, "You know Andi was such a gift to Mark in his grief. She saved him from drowning in it, maybe she can be that for you too. Let her lead you through this, let her be your reason. It doesn't matter why you survive, it just matters that you do."

"You're right, her existence is what has gotten me through this far. She is the most important person in this whole mess, and I need to remember that. It's only going to get harder and more complicated as she gets older. I can't shoulder it all alone, and I am grateful to you guys and Jack that I don't have to. I'm sorry I don't always show it, I just get so overwhelmed sometimes."

"It's okay, sis, I got you." He gives my shoulder an extra squeeze as my dad and Andi come through the other end of the barn.

I can't help the smile she brings to my face as I greet her. "Hey there, big girl! I've been looking all over for you."

"We were checking water; Grandpa says it's so hot it'll melt the wax off a mare's teat!"

Noah and I burst out laughing and our dad shrugs his shoulders. "What? It would."

"Come on, little miss, we gotta get home for dinner. Uncle Jack is meeting us at the house with your favourite pizza."

"Yes!" She shouts and pumps her fist in the air as she runs through the barn and across the farm to where my Jeep is parked.

I wave behind me as I follow her and call back, "Thanks for getting her from school, Dad, I'll see you tomorrow probably. Thanks for the chat, Noah, love you both."

They both call back their 'I love you's' as I follow Andi. It's so strange how often it's been Noah these days who knows the right thing to say to ease my worries. He's always been a great brother, but it's usually been Liam that took on the stereotypical role of oldest brother, Noah was always there for a laugh and a good time, while Liam was the one to hover over us and give advice. I need to remember that I'm not the only one changed by this grief. I guess he's becoming quite sage in his old age; if only I could believe everything that he keeps telling me. Life isn't always going to revolve around tragedy and grief. I can make room for love and happiness too.

These evenings with Jack and Andi leave my chest feeling so light with joy, it feels like I've never smiled or laughed this much in my life. I have, it's just been so many years that I've forgotten what it feels like. There is such a conflicting contrast because at the same time I feel like I'm on edge, like I'm just waiting for a wave to crash over me and send me back to where I was a few months ago.

We tuck Andi into her bed and Jack reads her her favourite story. Watching them melts my heart. She's snuggled in under his arm and he's too tall to fit the length of her bed, so his one leg hangs off the side where his foot sits on the floor and his other is on the bed. It looks highly uncomfortable, but he doesn't show it.

What will it do to her if this doesn't work out between us? What was I thinking letting him be so much a part of her daily routines? To be fair to myself, he already was 'Uncle Jack' long before we started anything, but it's been extreme the last few months. She's been so happy and thriving so much with his care and attention that I didn't want to see how much I could be screwing this up for her. As soon as she's asleep I need to talk to Jack and figure out a plan to slow things down. We need to just take a step back and make sure we're doing what's best for Andi and her fragile heart. I wait downstairs on the couch, wringing my hands together. I'm so frustrated that I missed this issue developing. I need to get this uneasiness off my chest. I can't afford to let it linger and fester and cause problems for Andi or for Jack.

Jack's voice interrupts my careening thoughts. "Hey, babe? What's going on? You look like you're freaking out!"

I huff out a laugh, damn him for being so observant. "I am. I am freaking out. I'm trying to...not... but it's not working."

He sits down beside me and gently takes my hands so they have no choice but to stop fidgeting. I ball them into fists, unable to even feel his gentle touch. It's sending my senses into overdrive when I feel like I'm already overstimulated by my thoughts running wild.

He looks to where I'm clenching my fists and sits back, giving me some space, then says, "Talk to me. Tell me what's going on in that beautiful head of yours."

I can't help but smile. This man is too good to me. Can he really be this perfect? Is he even capable of breaking my heart?

"I was watching you reading to Andi in her bed, and it sent me off on this downward spiral of craziness. I can't let her lose you. I can't set her up for that heartache again. I've been so focused on my heart and my feelings, and what I can handle but I've neglected to protect her." I'm breathing heavily from rambling without taking a breath.

He smiles and says, "You have to protect Andi from me? Big, bad Uncle Jack? Sar, what are you talking about? I would never hurt her. Or you. Ever. What is this really about?"

"I know you wouldn't on purpose, but what if we break up? What if something terrible happens to you? How can we put her through that again?"

He takes my hands again and I let him this time. He rubs his thumb over the pulse point on my wrist and I think I can feel it slowing just at his touch.

"Sar, what if something happens to you? Or anyone that she loves? It might happen. I pray to God that girl doesn't see another heartbreak until she's twenty-five and her first boyfriend breaks her heart, but the fact is, we don't have control over that. We have to just live our best lives with the time we're given, and for us, that means together. Side by side, we will get through anything this life throws at us. From here on out, it's the three of us against the world."

"It feels as childish as it sounds, but I have to protect my heart too. I can't let you in and fall head over heels and then have you ripped from me, whether by your own doing or by God's divine plan. I have zero tolerance for either of those things anymore. And did you say she's not having a boyfriend until she's twenty-five? That will never happen."

"Agree to disagree, but don't you get it, Sara? It's already done, you've already let me in, I'm right here! You've already fallen! I see it every day when you look at me with those gorgeous eyes. I feel it when you take my hand while we walk down the lane with Andi running ahead of us." He presses his lips to where his thumb is still gently rubbing my wrist. He makes his way up my arm with his lips. Goosebumps cover my body as he whispers, "I see it when you laugh at me trying to ride a damn horse just to make that little girl smile and to make your life a little easier. I see it when you're watching me snuggle in her bed and read her a story. I see you. All of you. I'm right fucking here and I'm not going anywhere, ever."

He steals the breath right from my lungs as he presses his lips to mine. I open for him like my life depends on it. His hands tangle in my hair, and I can't imagine being anywhere else in the world. Right here, with this man, is where I belong. I know it now, without a doubt. I will pick up the broken pieces of my shattered heart all over again, to be with him now and for as long as this world is willing to give us. I would do it all again.

I pull away gently and drag my lips across his jaw, the feel of his unshaven skin sending butterflies through my stomach. Reaching the crook of his neck, I rest my lips there and whisper, "I love you, Jack."

I can feel him smile into my hair as he whispers back, "I've loved you longer, Sara, but I love you more each day, and I'll love you and that little girl for as long as you'll let me."

His words send a shiver through my whole body, and before my lips join with his, I say, "Thank you for waiting." I keep saying it, even though I know, I will never be able to thank him enough.

CHAPTER
Fifteen

Jack

"Hey Charlie, what's a fifteen-year-old getting up to on a Friday night these days?" Noah hollers down the alley of the barn to where Charlie is putting the feed buckets away. He stuck around after spending time riding with Andi and I. He seems happy to help Noah and I give all the horses their grain and check water. Brent and Marie took Andi out to dinner while Sara is working late again. I could've just headed home for a cold shower but Noah volunteered to feed all the animals so his dad could take off, so I figured I might as well help too. I didn't expect Charlie to stay late and help out, but it got the job done even faster. He's splashing cold water from a pail onto his face, laughing in response to Noah's question.

"What's so funny? We're old but we're not that old. We know there's trouble to be had." I nod my head back to Noah. "Especially this guy, he was always causing shit in town when we were your age."

Charlie beams back to Noah. "No way, not Mr. Dreamboat Cowboy Firefighter over here?"

Noah barks a laugh. "Mr. Dreamboat Cowboy Firefighter came later in life. Shithead teenager was first."

I shake my head and ask again, "Seriously, what do you get up to? Do you have a group of buddies? I don't ever see you around town. It seems like you're always here."

His smile falls and I wish I could take it back. Maybe he doesn't have many friends. Or maybe he doesn't want to do anything but hang out here at the Ryan's. It is a pretty great place to be. It was one of my favourite places to be when I was his age, but this is where the guys my age were. If it wasn't for this place and Noah and Liam, I don't know what my teen years would've looked like. It seems odd that he's so happy hanging out with us old guys and Brent, who's a dinosaur compared to us. I'm about to retract my stupid question when he shrugs his shoulders and says, "Yeah, I have friends. Just a couple guys. We usually just hang out, have some drinks around a fire. They're not into horses and stuff though, so I've never brought them here."

Noah joins us and splashes water over his head to cool down. He pats Charlie on the shoulder and says, "Well not everyone understands this stuff but they're missing out." He turns and waves his hand in the direction of the pastures filled with grazing horses. "We're happy you're here, Charlie, and I know my dad really appreciates your help. Shit, I appreciate it because it keeps him off mine and Liam's backs to be out here helping more than we are."

We all walk back to the main drive to our trucks, laughing and chatting about the weekend. Charlie and Noah jump in Noah's truck and I slide in behind the wheel of my own. I sit and stare out at the horses in the fields, and I don't think I can remember a time I ever felt this carefree and happy. When I was a kid, I was always worrying about Kristen and how she was doing, and as a teen I worried about my dad and the farm creeped in. My twenties were a crash course on self employment and restoring the farm. Since Amy died, I've made a point to be available and be a support for the whole Ryan family, but especially for Sara and Noah. Even though the grief from losing Mark is fresh and feels like a knife in my gut sometimes, I feel like we've all learned to share the load. When I listen to Noah or

Sara hash out their emotions, it feels like I'm shouldering it for them and somehow that lessens my own. It gives the pain a purpose for me. I can be their person and heal myself through my relationships with them. Kristin would have a hay day with this concept. Fixer trauma response. Good thing she's not here.

My phone buzzes on the console before I pull out onto the main road. I see Sara's picture fill the screen along with a text.

Sara- *Dinner plans tonight? Mom and Dad have Andi.*

I smile because I'm one step ahead of her and already ordered take out to have at my place whenever she finishes up at work.

Jack- *Yeah, I have plans with some gorgeous woman, hoping she swings by so I can sweep her off her feet with my takeout ordering skills.*

Sara- *Haha! You're a real comedian. Good plan. Your ordering skills could use some practice. I will see you in 30 minutes.*

Jack- *Feel like staying the night? Or is Andi coming home later?*

Sara- *No she's having a sleepover. I will bring an overnight bag.*

I smirk before typing back.

Jack- *Or don't. (winky face)*

She leaves me on read. Jerk. She likes to just ignore me when she doesn't have a comeback. I'm fine with it. I know I won this round.

My arm is tingling and on the verge of losing all feeling, but I could watch this woman sleep until my arm fell off if she'd let me. I can barely remember how empty my life was a few months ago, my heart must have been as empty as my bed. Seeing her hair splayed across my pillow is enough to make my heartbeat quicken. The smell of her lavender shampoo lingers long after she's gone, and I can't get enough of it. I want to stay here forever with my body wrapped around hers, my fingers tangled in her long hair. All the shades of each strand are mesmerizing to me. My heart and soul belong to this woman, and the peace she brings me is something I've never felt before.

She sighs softly as I slide my arm out from beneath her. She rolls over into the spot where my body had just been, and I chuckle to myself as I stand from the bed to make my way to the bathroom. On my way back to my bedroom, back to Sara, something catches my eye out the window at the end of hall. It's bright enough that I go to the window to see what it could be.

"Fuck!" I yell as I run to my room to grab clothes. "Sara! Sara! Wake up! There's a fire outside! I don't know how far away it is— fuck, I have to get out there!" I dial 911 on my cell as I'm pulling a shirt over my head and grabbing an extra one. As I yell into the speaker giving the operator all the info she needs, Sara sits up in bed and flings her legs over the side. I shove my phone in my jeans pocket and head for the door.

"Whoa, what? Jack? What is going on? Slow down." She's groggy with sleep. I can't blame her, but I can't slow down. If that's as big as it looked from the window, I'm one breath away from losing everything.

"Sara, I have to go, there's a fire! The forest or something— I don't know!"

I run down the stairs and out the front door before she can respond. I grab my coat from the closet on my way by. It's hot as fuck out there, the hottest July we have on record, but I'm going to need something to protect me if this gets ugly, and when fire's involved, it always gets ugly.

It takes less than ten seconds for me to see that the fire is coming from the woods to the east of my property and it's encroaching on my trees faster than I could ever run. The most mature trees–ready for this Christmas–are on the eastern edge, getting younger as the rows head west. I try to push down the panic as I move as fast as my legs will carry me. I need to get to the barn to grab my chainsaw. All I can think to do is cut down as many rows as I need to, as far in as I can safely get at, and hope that it'll stop the fire. It could jump on the ground to the next rows, but I have to try something… anything. I try not to think of what will happen if this doesn't work. I focus on checking the fuel in the saw, grabbing gloves, and getting my ass into the field of evergreens. All I can smell is smoke and pine, well, burning pine specifically. Fuck! I can't believe this is happening! How did this happen? There's been a fucking province-wide fire ban since May!

I can hear the fire trucks coming down the road from town. I'm grateful for their fast response but I don't know if it'll be enough. Is there still a chance we can beat this before I lose my whole damn farm? I slow my pace as I reach the first rows of near mature pines, Noah is on one of those trucks and he will know what to do. He's known to be the wild card in his family, but he's always been grounding for me. I never thought it would mean so much to me to have a buddy on the fire department. God, I wish this wasn't my life right now. How quickly everything changed. It feels like years ago that I was lying in bed staring at Sara, imagining our future together, and now I'm watching it go up in flames. Literally.

I see movement out of the corner of my eye, and I turn towards it, worried Sara made her way out here. But when I turn to my left it's not Sara I see, but my mother. What the fuck? Have I already inhaled so much smoke that I'm already losing consciousness? I shake my head to clear my vision of what looked like my mother running through the rows of trees, only to see five-year-old me chasing after her, smiling and laughing. I didn't think I remembered her, but I know without a doubt that was her. I remember this day; it was the week before she died, we were playing hide and seek. We had just planted the flower bed at the edge of the field of pines. I watch those irises bloom every year and have never thought of the day I knelt in the dirt with my mother and felt the soil under my fingernails. If they survive this fire, I will think of her every time I look at them and I'll remember her love for me now. She was so young and healthy… and happy. Maybe this was the last time I was truly happy. And just like today it all came crashing down around me. The sound of Sara screaming my name jolts me out of whatever trance I was in.

"JACK! JACK!" She's getting louder as she approaches, running up behind me. Whatever that vision or memory was must have only taken a moment because the fire hasn't engulfed me or many more trees since I last looked ahead.

"Sara! Stay back!" I scream over my shoulder.

"Get out of there! What are you doing?" I can tell by her voice that she's frantic, but I can't worry about that now. I need her to stay somewhere safe.

As she runs up beside me, I see she has a scarf wrapped around her mouth and nose, thank God, but I yell, "Sara! I need to do this! This is my whole life! I can't be worrying about whether you're safe or not. Please stay back at the house!"

The fire trucks pull in the drive as I start backing away from her. "Please go tell them what's going on! See what they need!" I know that's a pointless task, but it will get her away from here and closer to the house. I make sure she's heading in the right direction before I turn to run back into the rows of trees. The smoke is so thick I can hardly see, and I know the fire isn't that close, but I can still feel the heat through my coat. I was sweating before but now it feels like I'm suffocating. The heat and smoke is overwhelming.

The trucks are on the edge of the field now. They need to get in here with some water to douse these trees. I know that will make all the difference. It's the only thing that will give my life's work a fighting chance. Without a second thought I start sawing through the row I'm standing in. I run as fast as I'm able, pushing my saw through each tree as low as I can. My arms are burning after ten or so trees, but I have ninety more. If I can get through these, I need to do another row. Hopefully that will be enough of a firebreak that I can save the younger trees behind me. Where are they with the fucking fire hoses?

I make it to the end of the row and start on the next one. From the end of the row I can see how much is already lost, so much fucking loss. I hear the spray of water when I'm only a few trees into cutting down the second row.

I hear someone holler, "We'll soak the ground along here, Jack! Keep going, we'll follow with the hose and douse the rest of the trees in the next few rows!"

I don't bother answering or looking back to see if Noah is there. I have to keep going, but the T-shirt I tied around my neck to cover my mouth and nose keeps falling. My eyes are burning, and my lungs feel like they're on fire too. I'm almost to the end of the row. If I can just finish this row, the fire might stop there. I will have done all I can.

Breathing heavily, I fall to my knees. Sara is beside me in a second. "Jack! Jack! Are you okay? Someone help! I need a paramedic over here! He needs help!"

My voice croaks. My throat is raw, either from screaming or from the smoke. "I'm... fine. Sara. It's... okay."

I try to lift my hand to her face; I want her to know I'm okay but the words coming out of my mouth aren't doing the greatest job of convincing her of that. I'm not injured though, I'm just exhausted and my chest is killing me, but no burns. She takes my hand in hers and pushes my hair from my eyes. Her touch feels like it could erase all the bad in the world right now. If only that were true. I don't know exactly what the loss is here tonight, but I know it's catastrophic. I know now, my life will never be what I once thought it could be. So much fucking loss. Plans, money, my whole future, so much time, all for nothing. I let Sara help me to my feet and we walk slowly to where the fire trucks, ambulance, and a couple police cars are parked. I sit on the step on the back of the ambulance as a paramedic checks my vitals and listens to my lungs. I should know her name; I went to high school with her brother, but I can't think straight. I need Sara. God, I'm so grateful she's okay. Everyone's okay. No one was hurt and that is a blessing I will focus on right now.

I croak to the woman checking me, "Where did Sara go?"

"I think she's looking for Noah. He was here but no one can find him at the moment..." She hesitates. "But I'm sure he's around here somewhere. People often get caught up in the chaos."

"What the fuck?! Noah isn't here?" My head is spinning, and it hurts like a sonofabitch, but where is Noah, why wouldn't he be right here? He wouldn't leave his sister's side at a time like this. I go to stand up and my vision swirls like I'm in a cyclone. I almost fall to the ground until strong hands grab me under my arms and plant my ass on a gurney, another familiar face that I can't quite place. "You're heading in to get checked out, Jack, no arguments." I'm about to argue when he throws an oxygen mask over my mouth and nose. "Smoke inhalation is serious stuff, brother. Take it easy, you'll be alright."

I'm fighting to get my bearings and get the damn thing off my face when Sara rushes to my side. I finally rip the thing off and can take her in like I couldn't before. Her swollen eyes are bloodshot and her cheeks are black with tear streaks running down them. Her hair is a tangled mess, either from running through the field of trees or because she was ripped from my bed by this fucking shit show.

I reach for her. "Sara, where is Noah?"

She chokes on a sob and throws her body against mine, her arms wrapping around my neck as her words shatter my world for the second time tonight.

"They don't know."

CHAPTER

Sixteen

Sara

I watch as the ambulance pulls out onto the road. Jack is in there. I keep watching as they take him further and further away from me. My heart is cleaved in two and there isn't a damn thing I can do about it. On one hand, every fiber of my being needs to be at Jack's side, to make sure he's okay and that all of his efforts to save his farm won't be all at the expense of himself. The other half of me is frantic to know where my brother is. No one saw him run into the blaze, but they all say he was on the truck when they arrived. How the fuck did he just disappear into thin air? My nerves are shot, and I want to break down but there just isn't time. I've been on the phone for what feels like hours, but I know it hasn't even been two hours since Jack woke me frantically yelling about a fire. How did everything get so messed up in such a short time? How many times in my life will I be left wishing I could go back to yesterday? How many times can a person be knocked down and keep getting back up? I am just so fucking tired.

My phone rings again. I look down expecting to see Liam's or my mom and dad's photo on the screen, calling with an update on Noah. Surely, he's contacted one of them by now! But there's no photo. It's Kristin. Shit. I don't even know what to tell her. She must know something, or she wouldn't be calling me at one in the morning. I hesitate for only another second and then swipe to answer. "Hey Kristin." My voice cracks even though I'm trying desperately to keep it even.

"Sara! Thank God I got a hold of you! Jack isn't picking up and someone posted on socials that there was a fire! My God! I've been freaking out trying to get a hold of him! Is it true? Was there a fire? Is he okay? The farm? Sara, tell me my brother is okay!"

"He's okay... I think he's okay. They told me he was." Tears run down my face again and I can't stop the sob that escapes my throat. Damn it! I didn't want to do this to Kristin. She shouldn't have to deal with me losing my shit right now.

"What do you mean, you think? Who told you?" She snaps at me, but I don't blame her. I can't sort my thoughts out enough for me to understand them, so I'm sure I'm not making much sense to her.

"I'm sorry, Kristin, I don't know for sure. Jack was okay but taken in an ambulance to the hospital to be checked more thoroughly. He inhaled a lot of smoke. There was a fire in the woods on the east side of the farm that caught some trees and spread to his fields. He cut down a couple rows to create a firebreak and the fire department arrived in time to douse the ground and trees there, so it worked. He lost a lot, but it could've been worse. The paramedic told me he would be okay and it was just a precaution to take him in and now—"

"Wait. Sara, why aren't you with him? You're at the farm? And you just let him leave to go to the hospital alone?"

"My brother is missing." I stop and take a breath, I force myself to swallow through the pain that is growing in my throat as I hold back my tears. "He was on the trucks when they arrived and now no one knows where he is."

"Oh my God, Sara, I'm so sorry. You must be a wreck; I knew something major had to be going on for you to leave Jack. Where is Andi?"

"She's with my parents. She was having a sleepover there tonight.

Nobody saw Noah run into the field of trees or the fire. They all went right to Jack and fought it from his firebreak. Some are still out there making sure it's out completely. We are all at a loss, and everyone's making calls and trying to find him. He has to be safe somewhere. I just can't imagine what would take him anywhere but here when Jack and I needed him."

"That is so bizarre. I'm on my way to the hospital though, so don't worry about Jack for now. Focus on your family and find Noah and find out what went on with him."

I pause as tears stream down my soot covered cheeks. My throat feels like it's closing now but I choke out, "Kristin... Jack is my family. I will be there as soon as I know that Noah is okay." I hang up before I break down completely. I cover my face with my hands, making an even bigger mess of it, I'm sure. As I pull my hands away, I notice another police car pulling in the driveway. It slows to a stop in front of the house and Noah steps out of the front seat. I rub my eyes with my gritty fingers and wince at the pain, but I can't imagine that I'm seeing this correctly. Noah just arrived at Jack's in a police cruiser when he arrived here hours ago in a fire truck.

I run to him so fast I almost trip over my own feet. I throw myself into his arms; the look of concern and worry on his face is so familiar. That combined with his arms around me might mean the end of my holding it together.

"Sara! What the fuck are you doing here? Where is Andi?" His voice is frantic as he rubs his hands down my back and starts patting my arms to check for injuries. His eyes are darting around the property, and he scans past the field of burnt tree carcasses to the barn–thankfully untouched–to the house behind us and then finally back to me. "Sara. Answer me. What are you doing here? You're covered in soot, you're a mess. What happened?"

"Andi is at the farm... a sleepover with mom and dad." I take a step back and run my fingers through my hair. I don't actually give a shit what I look like right now, but I need to do something with my hands. Now that he's safe and standing in front of me my fear is rapidly turning to anger. He wants to know what *I'm* doing here? Well, I want to know why *he* wasn't here. I stumble over my words but eventually get it all out. "I had dinner with Jack and stayed the night. He woke me up around midnight screaming there was a fire. He ran into it like a fucking mad man to save his damn trees and almost died in the process. He made me promise to stay back at the trucks to keep me safe. The trucks that my brother should have been on! Where the fuck were you? Where have you been this whole time?"

Noah rubs both his hands through his hair, hard and fast. His face is twisted into a look of pain and fear I don't know if I've ever seen on his face before. "Where is Jack now? Sara, please tell me he's okay."

I relay to him everything the paramedics told me. I want to get to him as soon as I can, but I still don't understand what would keep Noah from fighting a fire that was threatening his best friend's entire life's work. Fine, he didn't know I was here, but there's so many more questions he needs to answer.

"Noah, what happened to you? Where did you go once you got here? How? And why? I am so confused, and you need to help me understand."

He sits down on the front porch and lets his head fall into his hands, his shoulders slumping forward. I don't know if it's from relief or sheer exhaustion. He looks up at me with so much sadness emanating from him. "It was Charlie."

I am getting more confused by the minute. "What? What was Charlie?"

"The fire. It was Charlie Dawson and some guys from his school. They were back in those woods." He points to where the field of pines used to stand and the forest beyond. "They were drinking and thought it would be okay to have a small fire. One asshole kid dumped his bottle of liquor on it, and the flames shot up and caught a branch." He looks back to the burnt field again. "And you know the rest."

I'm shaking my head slowly trying to put together all the pieces to this story. Charlie Dawson, my dad's hired hand, the kid who rides with Jack and Andi! And he just burnt down half of Jack's crop?

I whisper, in a daze, "But there's a fire ban."

"Sara, come on, you know there's always idiots that ignore that. They think they're above our rules and safety guidelines. I just didn't think one of those assholes was Charlie. It isn't, actually. I know that. He's a good kid. I just don't know how to get him out of this."

"Wait, hold on. Get him out of it? Look at what they did!" I wave my hand towards Jack's ruined farm. "Where have you been, Noah? Please tell me you weren't helping that delinquent kid while Jack was fighting for his life." He pauses for too long before he answers me. "Please, Noah."

"I saw the cops grabbing them down the road. They were running from the trees just as they were driving by to come here. As soon as the trucks slowed, I jumped out and ran back. I saw that one of them was Charlie and had to make sure he was okay. He doesn't have a family like we had growing up and I know now he sure as hell doesn't have friends that are worth more than the shit on my shoe. He wouldn't have done this. Something happened, and he got caught up with some bad kids, I don't know. I know him, so do you, Sar. Come on, you know he wouldn't have been a part of something like this."

All I can do is shake my head, "I don't know him that well, I know he's kind to Andi and good with horses, that's it. I took dad's word for the rest of it. You're being naïve. He wouldn't have done this? How can you say that? Even if it was an accident, he fucked up. He's a kid and made a mistake, but that mistake cost a grown man his life's work and almost his life. I don't care what he got caught up in, Noah. It's not worth this!" I'm screaming at him now because I don't know what else to do. I can't believe he's so focused on this, on a kid that may or may not be a terrible person. Frankly, I don't give a shit if he is or not, I need to get to Jack. "I can't do this with you right now, I need to get to the hospital. I don't know how you'll face him when this is why you weren't here, fighting with him... for him. Fuck, Noah, you've really messed up this time."

My heart is suffering from serious whiplash. I've gone from fearing for Noah's life to wanting to throttle him for being so careless and selfish. I can't look at him another second, so I turn and run to my car and don't spare him another glance.

CHAPTER
Seventeen

Sara

I find Jack and Kristin sharing a gurney in a crowded hallway of the hospital. Seeing him sitting beside his sister and smiling as she talks makes my heart feel a little lighter. I've checked in with Mom and Dad and Andi is of course sound asleep. It's gotta be approaching dawn but everyone has been made aware that Noah is perfectly fine, and I will update them on Jack as soon as I talk to him.

I reach the spot where Jack and Kristin are sitting and softly interrupt their conversation, reaching for Jack's hand. "Hey hun, how are you feeling? What is the doctor saying?"

He looks up, surprised to see me, but also relieved I think, I hope. Before I can question it too much, he pulls me between his legs that are dangling off the gurney, nearly pulling me onto his lap. His strong arms wrap around me, and my nose is filled again with the smell of smoke and ash. I had changed my sweater before I came inside and didn't realize the relief such a small change had brought. My jeans and hair are still disgusting but it's so much stronger on Jack's clothes.

"You're okay? Is Noah alright?" He mumbles into my neck.

"Yeah, I'm fine, Jack, I was always fine. You made sure I stayed safe." I hold his face with my hands and kiss his lips gently. "I'm more worried about you. Noah's fine, never mind about that right now. What are they saying? Are they admitting you or can you come home?"

"I can go if my chest X-ray comes back clear. I'm just waiting for the doc to come tell me either way. Where was Noah? Where is he now?"

I forgot Kristin was sitting beside us until she said, "If Noah is fine then where was he? He was at the farm with the fire department, and then just wasn't?"

"It's a long story, but yeah, he was there and then left, but he's fine. I don't really want to talk about it. I look back at Jack. "I'll tell you everything when we get out of here."

"We have time to kill. Just spill it, Sara, what's going on?"

I rub my face with my hands, the smell of burning pines embedded in my skin. I can't get away from it. I want to cry thinking about everything Jack lost tonight and at the hands of some stupid teenagers. It's just so stupid, I could scream. I can't imagine how he's going to react when he finds out, but I guess he's right; now or later, really makes no difference in the end.

I sigh heavily. "He came in on the trucks with the whole crew, but he saw the cops just down the road and some kids running out of the woods. They were being arrested or questioned, I don't know—"

"Wait. What? Kids started the fire? Why would anyone want to light my farm on fire?" He's shaking his head incredulously trying to make sense of something that will never make sense.

"They didn't want to. They were just in there hanging out, hiding from any suspicious eyes I assume, since they were drinking and had a fire going. It caught a low branch and that was all it took. It moved fast and caught your field of trees as soon as it cleared the woods."

Kristin is clenching and unclenching her fists as she says, "Jack lost his livelihood and our family's legacy because some teenagers made a bad decision? There's been a fire ban for months!"

"I know, I know." I'm trying to control my anger, but my hands are shaking. It's just so unfair and I can't stand this feeling of knowing there's nothing I can do to make any of this better.

Kristin interrupts my thoughts again. "Hold on, why was that more important to your brother than fighting for Jack's farm? Why would he leave his best friend and his *sister* in the middle of a crisis to see about some fucking kids? A crisis that he's trained to fight! He's a Goddamn fire fighter!"

I hate that she's voiced my exact thoughts, because that's pretty much the exact thing I said to Noah not even an hour ago, but it stings a little coming from someone else. I want to jump to defend him, but I have no defense, because it doesn't make sense to me either.

I lower my eyes and stare at my hands. I can't stop twisting and squeezing them, trying to stop them from shaking, I can't look at Jack, I don't want to see if he has the same look of burning rage that his sister has. Finally, quieter than I intended, I say, "He didn't know I was there. He thought I was at home with Andi, like I usually am." As soon as the words are out of my mouth, I regret them.

Kristin explodes, throwing her hands in the air as she jumps off the gurney and spins around to glare at me. "Well, excuse me! His precious sister wasn't there so he didn't give a shit about my brother? His best friend? What the fuck, Sara! What does that even mean? He didn't care enough to do the job that he's paid to do. I'm not even expecting him to go above and beyond, just fucking show up to work and do your job!"

Jack growls and says between gritted teeth, "Kristin, will you shut up and sit down?"

Spoiler alert, she doesn't.

"What? Jack. You can't be serious right now? How are you not punching a hole in this wall?" She waves her hand to the cinderblock wall behind us. "Or at least trying to? How are you so calm? He abandoned you in your greatest time of need."

"He must have had a good reason."

"That's it?" Kristin screeches. "That's all you have to say? You're fine with the fact that because he didn't know *Sara* was there, he just fucked off to do something he deemed more important."

"Don't use that tone when speaking Sara's name." His eyes are hard and unmoving when he makes eye contact with her, the brown is so dark I can't make out his pupil. "Of course, I'd expect him to drop anything and everything for her, I would too, and I would for you! I have no doubt that would have changed his course of action, but he didn't know she was there, and I kept her safe so, what the fuck are you getting at?"

She shakes her head and shoves her hands into her jeans pockets as she storms away. She tosses over her shoulder from halfway down the hall, "I'm going to find coffee."

I don't want to, but I remove myself from Jack's grip and hoist myself up beside him. I rest my hand on his thigh, unable to not touch him, "Jack. I'm so sorry, she's not wrong. I can't believe Noah did this."

"Sara, tell me what you know. What was the deal with the kids? Why did he care enough about that to leave fighting the fire to the rest of the department?"

I close my eyes; it doesn't tame the fury but I'm trying. Why does it hurt so much more to know that someone we know was involved in this? Someone I trust with Andi's life. Riding thousand-pound animals is no small feat and I've trusted him to do it with her. Fuck, I wish I could make this make sense in my head before I have to tell Jack, but I can't, and I don't know if I ever will.

"He saw Charlie."

I don't even have to look at his face. I can hear in his voice that his brow is furrowed and he's screwing up his mouth in confusion when he says, "What do you mean? Where?"

"The kids ran from the woods, unknowingly towards the police. He saw that one of them was Charlie. He said he had to go see what happened and make sure that he was okay. He keeps saying that he wouldn't have done this. He wanted to help him somehow, I guess, I don't really know. I'm so sorry, babe, I don't know what he was thinking, or how that took precedence in his mind even for a second, but it's done and that's why he did it."

He doesn't respond for too many long moments. I finally chance a look at him, and his face is expressionless. I take his hand in mine again. "Jack? Honey? Are you alright? You look a little pale again."

He doesn't move but he says, "I'm fine."

"What are you thinking? Can I do anything?"

He slowly turns and looks at me, his eyes are softer now, but still so serious and tired. More than tired– exhausted–but they still see right to my soul when he looks into mine. Finally he says, "He's right, you know."

Now I'm confused. "Who?"

"Noah. Charlie wouldn't have done this. I get that you're saying he was there, but guilty by association is bullshit. There's more to it. I want to talk to him."

"You can't be serious. Jack, come on! These kids will only get slapped on the wrist as it is, and you think you need to waltz in and be the hero to your own villain. Give me a break. Please don't put yourself through this when you have so many other problems right now, problems caused by this kid, I might add."

"Something like this could ruin that kid's entire future in this town. I know that's not who he is. He's a good kid with a tough past, but I'll be damned if I let one night with the wrong guys ruin his future."

I don't want to rub salt in his wounds, but I can't figure out why these guys are so set on helping this kid when we have our own shit to deal with, it's like they're delusional or something. "Jack, you do understand how much you lost of your own future tonight, don't you?"

"I've been sitting here all night thinking about how I'd lost everything, and how my life and future were ruined. But when I looked up and saw you standing here in front of me, being able to pull you into my arms, hearing you tell me Noah wasn't hurt, I realized that I didn't lose everything. My life isn't ruined, the trees are ruined, yes, but they are not my life." He chuckles before he goes on, actually chuckles... has he lost his mind? "Obviously, money is good, and I don't know what this will mean for my business, but it's just money, Sar. You are everything to me. Andi is tucked safely into bed at your parents', and you are here by my side. That is all that matters. I know I'll be okay, the farm will be okay. We've got this... together."

CHAPTER
Eighteen

Jack

The doctor released me from the hospital with strict instructions to return if I experience any pain or shortness of breath. I'm back home, in my bed, twenty-four hours since the last time I was here. Sara is once again in my arms and I'm stricken by how much has changed in those last twenty-four hours, and yet how much has stayed the same. I wasn't kidding when I told her I was focusing on what I have, not what I lost. I know it's hard for her to wrap her head around. She's been drowning in grief for so many years, I'm sure she can't help but be swallowed by it again. I know I'm her life raft, and I won't sink under the weight of this. I will hold strong to the positivity that has kept me going for the twenty-six years that have passed since my mom died. I know there's some underlying reason why I saw her running through the trees while they were burning to ash, but I won't dwell on that right now. I'll talk to 'therapist Kristin' after some time passes and she lets go of all this anger she's directing at the world. Actually, not at the world, mostly just Noah.

We spent the day at Sara's with Andi, revelling in the happiness that she emanates, even when we're wrecked from this thing called life. I talked to Noah, but he didn't give me any more details about what's going on with Charlie than what Sara already did. I told him to pass on to him that we need to talk, and that I'm not pissed at him. I know he's probably scared shitless and won't want to see me, but I don't want him to feel that way. I want to know where things went wrong with him and how we can help.

Tomorrow will be spent here, working in the field. I asked Brent to borrow his tractor; it's a lot larger than mine and can push over and pull out whatever remains of my field. At a glance I estimate I lost about four thousand trees, all of this year's crop and most of next year's too. All that's left untouched are trees that are much too young to sell anytime soon. Insurance will cover the ones I lost but that'll need to go towards buying semi-mature trees to replant. It won't help me survive through this year and most of the next without selling a single Christmas tree. I don't know if my contracts will return after two years of needing to find another supplier. I feel like I'm starting over. Again. I already fucking did this once. God dammit!

I won't let myself spiral into those thoughts. It's fine. I'm fine. Sara and Andi are safe. She's here in my arms, right where I need her to be. She didn't want to leave Andi another night, but she wouldn't leave me either, then Andi begged to stay with Brent and Marie so that made her decision easier. Hers is a love I will never let go. I won't let this crisis drag me down, I can handle it. I just have to be strong for her. I don't know what I'll do if I lose her now after everything. If she thinks this is too much, or if she falls back into her fear of me dying or getting hurt or worse, leaving her. I don't know if I'll be able to pull her out of it a second time. There are so many possibilities, millions of ways for us to fail. The 'us' part still feels fragile.

I can't stop thinking about everything that will need done, and I can't stop staring at her beautiful face. Finally, only in sleep, does she look peaceful. This woman is my peace, I wonder if she knows that. My mind wanders to thoughts of my mother, not for the first time since I saw her running through the fire. I feel like she was trying to tell me something, but that sounds a little woohoo. I bet even Kristin would think so. The fire didn't make it to my mother's flower bed, but I wasn't too worried, knowing they'd grow back anyway. They grow again every year, just as beautiful, no matter what befalls them in the months between.

That thought gives me hope.

Maybe everything will come back as beautiful as it was, or even better... just like Sara did. She rose above her grief and is so much stronger and more confident than I've ever seen her, and she amazes me everyday. My muscles feel like they're wound like a top, and my throat still hurts like a bitch, but I feel lighter with her here. She is my hope and my reason. I will fix this, I have to. For her.

I get up and scribble her a note, I leave it under her water glass on her bedside table so it's the first thing she'll see when she wakes up. Even if I'm not here, I want her to know.

This is it, we made it.

I don't know if the assurance is more for her or for me, but either way, I need to remember. I have everything I've always wanted, right here. I fall asleep with that pressing on my mind and my heart.

Noah shows up first thing the next morning with Charlie in the front seat of his truck, Sara scowls and heads right back inside to join Kristin where she's eating breakfast. I hope they'll both come around to see the bigger picture here. I don't blame Noah for being worried about a kid before me, how can I hold that against him? And as for Charlie, I just need to talk to him before I pass judgement on what happened that night.

Noah hops out of his truck and ambles towards me. He's lost his large, confident aura that usually follows him everywhere. He looks nervous and unsure, and to make that even more obvious, he reaches his hand out to shake mine when he gets to me. I grab his outstretched hand and use my other arm to pull him into me as it wraps around him. This man is like a brother to me, and I won't stand by while he carries this burden of guilt on my behalf.

"I'm so sorry, man," he says over my shoulder.

"Nothing to be sorry for, brother. You did what you had to do." I smack his back to let out some of the emotion starting to clog my throat.

He pulls away and waves his hand to the field that used to be lined with perfectly pruned Christmas trees and is now charred black, with rows of scorched trunks. "But this—" His voice cracks as he cuts off whatever he was going to say.

"It'll be okay. We'll figure it out, we always do."

He smirks, finally looking a little like himself. "Listen to you, always the optimist." He nods his head back in the direction of where he parked his truck. "Charlie doesn't want to be here. He's ashamed and scared and feels like his life is over. How are you feeling about talking with him?"

"I'm good, I think it's important. I don't want this to ruin his reputation here, but I want to know what went down. How did he end up with those guys?"

"He needs to tell you that story himself, but Jack, you know he didn't have much of a rep before, Dad's the only one who's ever given him the time of day."

"Yeah, that's kinda what I mean. With Brent on his side, he could've made out alright despite his parents screwing up their lives, and his, all over the countryside. I thought he was starting to rise above it. Anyway, yeah, I want to talk to him. Thanks for bringing him over."

Noah glances from the truck back to my front door, the fear on his face towards the women inside my house is almost comical.

I laugh lightly. "You going in?"

"Do I have to?"

"Yup, they're both in there. Fair warning."

He runs his hands through his hair, making it stand on end more than it already was. "Fuck." He draws out that word just like he's drawing out going inside. He looks back at me, "Kristin's in there too?"

"Yup." I punch the side of his arm on my way by. "Best of luck, see you on the other side."

He calls after me, "Hey! I helped you win over Sara, what the fuck man! Help me with your sister now!"

"Oh no, you crossed Kristin in the worst way. She thinks you've done me wrong; I don't know if there's any coming back from that. She's fiercely protective of her people."

I hear him mumble something that sounds a lot like a string of curses as he makes his way to my porch. I smile and can't help a little laugh as I make my way to his truck to see Charlie.

I hop into the driver's side of the truck and shut the door. I don't plan on going anywhere but maybe sitting side by side instead of having to face me will make this easier on the kid. I glance over to him and he's staring down at his hands. They're clasped so tightly that his knuckles are white. His face is pale, and I can see that his eyes are puffy–wait, not puffy, swollen. His right eye is swollen and black and blue. What the fuck?

"Charlie. What happened to your face?"

Silence.

"Charlie, look at me."

He lifts his head but doesn't turn towards me. His face crumples as he covers it with his hands. "I'm so sorry, Jack, I'm so sorry." His shoulders start shaking, and I know he's doing his best not to cry in front of me.

"We'll figure it out, kid, just tell me what happened. How did you end up with those guys? I know you're better than the shit they were getting up to."

He shakes his head hard like he can shake the memories out of his head. "I don't know, it was stupid. I'm so sorry this happened to you. I mean... I wouldn't... I hate that it happened at all. But man, to you of all people. You and Noah have always treated me like one of the guys, like a real person. And now this... I'm so dumb, I'm so sorry."

"Hey, hey, hey. It's okay, don't say you're dumb, you did something dumb, but that thing… it doesn't define you. We've all made bad choices. We don't all have being fifteen years old as an excuse either, but it will be okay. You can help with all the work that's going to have to get done around here in the next few months, but more than that I want to know how you got mixed up in it in the first place. If you want forgiveness you have to be able to tell me what you're apologizing for. You're sorry it happened, but what would you have done differently if you'd known this would be the outcome?"

His eyes widen and before he can think about what he's saying he tells me exactly what I want to know, "I wouldn't have given them my dad's liquor! I would've told them to fuck off from the beginning and they wouldn't have been able to hold it over my head that I stole from my dad. I would know I don't want friends like them anyway, and I wouldn't have cared if they beat the shit out of me. I would've told Noah what they wanted; he could've helped me. I should've told them I was friends with Noah Ryan, and then they would've been too scared to mess with me." He looks down at his hands in his lap again. "Please don't tell my dad. He's too drunk to notice a couple bottles missing but he'll hit me harder than those assholes did if he finds out."

"The guys you were with the other night did that. I pointed to his eye, "Even after you did what they wanted?"

"Yeah, because I told the cops and then Noah too, that I was only with them because I stole the liquor and they threatened to rat me out for it. They wanted me to go down with them if they got caught. I guess I ratted myself out, but I don't want anyone thinking I wanted to burn down your farm! Or that I was dumb enough to light a fire during a fire ban, I tried to stop them, I swear I did! But they wouldn't listen, and I couldn't take them all on. I'm so sorry, Jack."

"I know you are." I move to get out of the truck, and he stares at me in disbelief. I give him a small smile, and there's nothing else to say. I have my answers. "Well, let's go, we have a shit ton of work to do and you're going to be my right-hand man until it's done."

He jumps out of his side of the truck and runs around the front of the truck to stand in front of me, holding his hand out to shake mine. "I'll do anything, whatever it takes."

"I wish you guys would quit trying to shake my damn hand. Come 'ere kid."

I grab him to pull him in for a hug, I ignore the surprised look on his face and how tense his body feels, like he's never been hugged in his life. Growing up without a mom and having an emotionally distant father could have had me being the same way, but I wanted Kristen to know what a loving home felt like. I wanted her to feel hugs and kisses and physical affection, so I learned as I was growing up to give that to her whenever I could. This kid has a mom and a dad, but I have a feeling they haven't been around much to show him affection of any kind.

CHAPTER Nineteen

Jack

Brent brought over his tractor and plow and Charlie's been working all week to clear the rubble of burned trees and turn the dirt to prepare it to plant new ones. Noah and I roadtripped yesterday to buy three thousand five-year-old trees. It's going to screw up my numbers when they all mature, but I can't risk seedlings or yearlings in this weather. It's so damn dry and even with turning the earth as much as Charlie is, I don't think many would survive. The older they are, the higher my chances of success. It feels like a huge risk even doing it this way, but I have to do something.

Sara has given up her wrath towards Charlie and Noah, thanks to Andi I think. She's been over here everyday after school helping in any way a seven-year-old can. She rides in the tractor with Charlie or helps unwrap all the new trees so they're ready to plant. I haven't had much time alone with Sara, since she's still working herself to the bone at the newspaper and running Andi around when she needs to be somewhere. When she's not doing all that she's here, helping me put this place back together. I'm staring into space thinking about how much I miss the lazy days we had before the fire, when Kristen appears on the front porch of the house. She's been staying here while she's in town like she usually does, but she doesn't usually stay this long. I'm not complaining; I love having her here, but I do wonder what's going on with her. I walk over to the porch and sit on the step, motioning for her to join me. She clumsily plops down beside me and sighs heavily.

"What's up, sis?"

"I don't know, Jack. I don't know what I'm doing anymore."

"What do you mean?"

"I mean, I don't want to leave. I don't want to leave you with this mess, but I hate that I wasn't here when it happened. I just feel like the hour drive is too far all of a sudden. I can work in any hospital, or doctors' office even, I went into nursing knowing I'd have options, yet I haven't moved from exactly where I landed after graduation. I guess... I think I want to move back."

"Holy shit, Kristin, that's amazing! Isn't it? Why do you seem like there's an issue?"

She looks at me out of the corner of her eye before she says, "I didn't know if you'd want me back, inserting myself in the middle of this life you're creating here."

"What? That makes no sense. You are my life, Kristin, you and me, always. You know that."

"But you have Sara now, and Andi. And I love that for you, but since I've been gone, so much has changed. Where do I fit here anymore?"

"You fit wherever you put yourself. I'll be honest and say I don't want to be your permanent roommate, but I would love you living close by again," I tease. "We can hangout and I can get free therapy whenever I want."

She smacks my arm as she says, "Like you don't already get that over the phone on a weekly basis."

I bark a laugh, and throw my hands up in defense. "Not denying it, but seriously, do whatever is best for you. If you want to be close by, get your ass over here. If you're happy living and working in Alton, then stay there. Only you can decide."

"I know, and I think I have decided. I was just worrying about your reaction, but I guess that was dumb." She leans over and rests her head on my shoulder.

"Yeah, really dumb," I lean away, anticipating that she's going to smack me again. It's futile though, she gets me anyway. I wrap my arm around her and pull her in close. I want to make sure she knows how much I love her but it also prevents any more physical blows. I decided now is a good time to tell her about what I saw, or remembered, when I was running towards the fire. She stays silent for a long time, then says, "That's super weird, Jack. I thought you didn't remember her at all?"

"I know, I didn't think I did either. But I know that was a memory, because it was as familiar to me as if it was yesterday. Seeing her felt like losing her all over again. I remembered how sad I was that she wasn't able to hug me anymore or tuck us in at night. I don't think I've felt that sadness over all these years but when faced with the possibility of losing everything, that's what came rushing back."

"That's so crazy. I think you need to talk about her more. You're always helping me and listening to me, but you never share your own shit about Mom, or Dad for that matter. He left a hefty weight for you to carry, and you just carry it with a smile. It's okay to be pissed off sometimes, you know. We got dealt a shitty hand and no offence, but yours was worse than mine. I had you, who do you have?"

"I had you too, Kristin."

"No, I was just another job for you. Another task to check off– hold on! Don't freak out, I'm not saying that I don't mean more than that to you, but you function by fixing things and helping people and that's the need I met for you. I won't deny that I needed you, and you were there for me, always. I am forever grateful to you for everything you did for me growing up but maybe it's time you look at that and focus on yourself now." She looks out over the farm and in a teasing tone says, "Look at this place! It could really use your attention, it's wrecked! Destroyed actually."

"Okay, okay, thanks for that, Captain Obvious."

She laughs. "What I mean is, you have three people here helping you. Liam and Sara come when they can, same with Brent, but you're rebuilding this place from the ground up again, with Noah and Charlie and whatever measly help I am. That's it. It doesn't have to be this way. Ask for help! This whole town would pour in here to help you if they knew you needed or wanted them to."

"I hear you, it's just not that easy. I can't help that I want to help people, that's not going to change, Kristin."

She stands up and laughs. "I don't want that to change, Jack. It's what I love most about you, but let others be that for you too. Don't ignore Mom's memory or your grief about her death. Maybe you can relate to Andi a little bit. I'm sure she'd love to hear about Mom, and you can talk to her about Amy since she doesn't have memories of her."

"You know, I never thought of that. I don't have a lot of specific memories of Amy either, but just like with Mom, I know she was a great person and had a huge heart. Maybe she would like hearing about our mom, and feel less alone in her own loss."

"You're catching on, big brother." She turns to walk towards the barn but quickly spins back towards me, and growls, "Incoming," as she beelines it into the house and slams the door behind her. With her out of the way, now I see Noah crossing the yard, heading this way.

"What is with her?" he says, shaking his head in disbelief. "You'd think I carried the plague or something."

I laugh because that was weird, but Kristin is weird, so I don't think much of it.

"She holds a grudge, I guess. How are you still here anyway? Don't you have to work?"

He rubs his hand across the scruff on his chin. "Ah yeah... about that... no, I don't have to work."

I don't even bother trying to hide my confusion. "Why not? You didn't use vacation time for this, did you?"

"Not exactly." He kicks the dirt around on the ground with his boots. "I got suspended."

"What?" He must be kidding. He's not laughing but he also isn't as upset as he should be if this was true, so what the fuck is going on?

"Yeah, for leaving the scene. It was a shit thing to do. I wasn't really thinking straight, and I know we've worked it out, but Chief isn't as forgiving as you. Nor should he be. That could've ended so much worse, for everyone. I really fucked up."

I shake my head. "Wow. For how long?"

"That's the real kicker. I quit."

"Noah, holy shit! I'm sure you can tell Chief it was a mistake; you were just pissed off and worried about this place."

"Nah, it wasn't that. Facing the forced time off and thinking about the choice I made that night made me realize that my heart isn't in the job anymore. I joined because Mark and I had this big grand plan to fight fires together, raise our families living side by side, spend our days off together with our wives and kids, retire together on Dad's farm. It all slipped away with him, and I don't want any of it if I can't have all of it."

"Shit. I'm sorry, man, that makes sense. I just didn't know you were feeling that way about the department."

"I didn't really either. Everything these last couple weeks has just put everything in perspective. I didn't even really care when the Chief told me I was suspended. That was kind of a red flag." He chuckles and I can tell he's at peace with his decision. Now that I know all this has been going on, I can see how he's been different, but then also more himself, this week more than ever. Like he's finding himself again, even though Mark isn't here to do life with. I can't help my curiosity, so I ask the question replaying in my mind. "What are you going to do now?"

He smiles now, bigger than I've seen since he was conspiring to trick Sara into going on a date with me. "That, my friend, is where you come in! Come check something out in the barn with me." This guy clearly gets off on scheming. I have a feeling this time involves me more than I'm bargaining for.

We're standing in my barn; Noah's looking around, side to side and up at the ceiling, to the back wall and then to the big double doors we just walked through. I don't know what he's thinking, but I really love it in here. He's making me take notice of the space. Since it's been completely cleaned out, when I took over the farm, I made this into a space that screamed cozy Christmas celebrations. We cleaned and sealed the concrete floor and hung strings of twinkle lights all over the walls and from the ceilings. There are garlands of pine and cedar strung throughout too. I leave it all up year-round because it's never used for anything else in the offseason. I made a bar from old beams I found in the rafters. It's perfect to have someone serving hot chocolate and cookies to customers. There's a little stage at the back of the open room where we set up a fancy chair and sleigh for Santa to do photo ops with kids and families. All of this has made all the difference over the years, attracting new clients from beyond Balsam River, because they can turn getting a Christmas tree into a whole family event, and it still only costs as much as the tree. I don't charge extra for all of this; once it is done up, it only costs me the wages of the couple of people working it. I more than recover that in the mass amounts of customers that it attracts.

"Okay, what's put that goofy smile on your face?"

He swipes his hand across his mouth. "I don't have a goofy smile, I only have one smile and it's irresistible and charming."

I bark out a laugh. "If you say so." Sarcastically, I add, "I can hardly resist you, now tell me what you're scheming about in my barn."

He claps his hands together and exclaims, "I want to buy into Balsam Trees."

I look at him incredulously. "Why? It's kind of in shambles right now, but even when it isn't, it doesn't earn enough to keep us both afloat. What are you thinking?"

"I want to buy in, and then open Balsam's Brewery. Right here, in this barn. Cool right? What do you think?"

I can't hide my shock, but also, it is a cool idea. I've never thought of using the barn for anything else, mostly because I don't have the time. But if Noah ran it and invested his money to make it happen, this could be next level.

"Are you sure this is what you want to do? How do we know it'll make enough money to make it worth it?"

He rubs his hands together excitedly. This is so funny, seeing him like this. I love that he's excited, but I want to make sure he knows what he's getting into, getting us both into.

"Yes! I've been to enough microbreweries that I know they're insanely profitable, but combined with this rustic feel and the Christmas atmosphere, it'll make the tree sales go through the roof again and give us revenue in the offseason." He points to the back corner, to the right of where I have the bar. "That whole area can be where we produce and bottle, and then we can serve it from the bar and set up tables for people to sit and hang out. We can leave the stage where it is but use it for live music when it's not Christmas. Shit, we could put a band up there with Santa's sleigh in the winter months too. What do you think, Jack? Come on, it's a great idea! I can see your gears turning!"

"I do think it's a great idea, but how much will it cost to get up and running, and how long until it's turning a profit? Is now the best time to be doing this when I'm already going to be behind the eight ball?"

"This is the best time. These next couple years were going to be shit for you, but with this they won't be! I have the money saved, I've been investing for years, and now I can invest in this."

I furrow my brow. "I don't know, it feels a lot like you're putting your life savings on the line to save my business. Fuck that, Noah, I'm not your charity case."

"Hey, hey! That's not what this is. I want equal shares in the trees too. I want to do this together and we'll make each other a killing. I need to find something to do with my life that I will enjoy but will also make me money, and I know this is it! I need you as much as you need me right now and that's the best way to go into business. Tell me I'm wrong."

I raise an eyebrow and shake my head. "You could be wrong."

"But I'm not. This is the ticket, Jack; it's going to be awesome!" I smile at how much he's acting like a teenage boy who just found his first beer. "Let me talk it out with Sara before I commit, but yeah, okay, it does sound pretty awesome."

Maybe he's right, maybe this is what could save me from the ruin I thought this fire would bring to my business. It's not something I could ever do on my own, but if I can just let him in, to work his 'Noah magic', it could change everything.

CHAPTER
Twenty

Sara

I'm meeting Kristen and Jenna at Liam's for breakfast today. I love that Kristen has just fallen right into our group without any hesitation. She walks through the doors just as I'm taking my seat at our back corner table. I wave her over and she smiles as she heads to the counter to order. When she comes to sit down, I can see how exhausted she looks. Her eyes have dark circles beneath, and her colour seems a little off. I haven't seen her much this week because I've been busy working, which is frustrating as hell when I know Jack needs my help at the farm. I know she's been helping him out a lot while she's waiting to hear back from Balsam Memorial about a job she applied for. I'm happy for both her and Jack that she's staying in town. I think he'll really love having her around again and I know I'd be lost without my big brothers so I can imagine she's missed him while she's been living out of town.

She reaches down for a side hug and then slips into the chair beside me. "Hey Sar, how's it going?"

"I was just about to ask you the same thing. You look wiped, beautiful but exhausted."

She laughs. "Ha! That could not be more accurate. I can't believe how much doing physical labour every day is taking me out! I should be embarrassed but honestly, I'm too tired to care."

"I hate that I can't be there. I don't know how much I could do, but I'm sure it would take a bit of the load off." I pause and twirl my hair nervously at my side. "You know, I've been tossing up quitting at the paper for awhile now, and I think this might be the last shove I need to take the leap. Jack needs me and I'm so tired of not being able to be there for him."

I notice the look of shock on her face, like she thinks I'm crazy. "Are you serious? Sara, that's huge."

"It is and it isn't. Jack and I talked about it months ago. I've always wanted to write for myself, maybe a novel, or several, someday. Mark and Amy wanted someone–in their plans it was Amy of course–but someone home with Andi or available to her for all her things. Mark's will made it possible for me to do that, and I've just been turning it over in my head. If I think I can actually do it, can I be an author?"

"Of course you can, you're an amazing writer! Jack never mentioned any of this to me so I was just caught off guard. You should definitely do this if you think it's best for you and Andi. She's so lucky to have you. I know how much I would've loved an aunt like you around when I was growing up, and Andi not only has you but Jenna too. I'm just so happy for her that she'll have that female support and role models. I can already tell that you put her first if you're quitting your job to support her better."

Of course, Jenna chooses that moment to plunk down in the chair opposite me. The girl has the worst timing, or the best she'd say.

"What?" she squeals. "You're doing it? You're going to quit."

I smile and shake my head. "Yeah, I guess I am. I didn't really know that when I woke up this morning, but the timing feels right, and I want to be able to be around more for Andi and support Jack in rebuilding the farm in any way I can."

"What do you think your parents will say? I know Liam and Noah will have your back; they've been riding me for months wondering what you were going to do." She rolls her eyes. "Dumbasses are too afraid to ask you."

We all laugh. "You're probably not too far off. I tore a strip off Noah a while back for hounding me. He was just trying to be supportive but between the two of them and my parents, he took the brunt of it when I was finally fed up." I can't hide my wince when I think of telling my parents. "They're definitely going to have to take some time to get used to the idea. They like the concept of predictable and steady income. They know it's not necessary with how Mark set things up for Andi and I, but it doesn't matter because they think they know what's best. I know they mean well, but ugh! I could use a break from them being all up in my business."

Jenna smiles and lifts her coffee to the center of the table. Motioning for us to do the same, she leans in and says quietly, "We got your back, girl, we know you've got this!"

We laugh and clink our mugs together and my heart feels a little warmer and a little lighter. It feels good to have finally made a decision, and it feels amazing to know I have friends and family who will support me.

After we catch up with each other about the daily comings and goings of each other's lives, Kristin starts to fiddle with her mug and spoon and all of a sudden seems uneasy. I rest my hand over hers, stilling the spoon from tapping. "Hey, are you okay?"

She doesn't look up when she answers. "I don't know. I have an idea, but I don't know how well it will go over with Jack."

I laugh and yank my hand away. "Oh boy, I don't know if I should be involved in this then."

Jenna smirks, always the optimist, and tries to convince me otherwise before she even knows what Kristin is talking about., "Oh, I'm sure it's not that bad. What's this about, Kristin?"

"It's about the farm and helping him plant the trees. They've finally got all the burned trees cleared and the rubble either loaded up and taken out or turned under. The kid has the ground almost ready, so Jack said we'll start digging holes this weekend. Three thousand holes! It's already August, and it'll take us well into September if we don't have help. And he thinks he has help. Well, I'm sorry, it takes me a long ass time to dig a hole big enough for one of those trees, then to put it in and fill it in. I wouldn't want to time myself, but I'm not the help he needs."

Jenna bursts out laughing while I stifle my own laughter with my hand covering my mouth. "You're not wrong, Kristen. He has Noah, Liam and Charlie, and my dad will help when he can too, but you're right. He'll be weeks doing it that way. So, what's your idea?"

She looks at me cautiously. "Could you talk to everyone that's willing to help from around town, like Noah and Jack did back when he first took over the farm from our dad? Back when Noah wasn't a selfish prick."

"Hey, hey, sister present. Be nice!"

"And sister-in-law," Jenna says., "What is your issue with Noah anyway? He's not a bad guy."

Kristen rolls her eyes. "I know, I guess I just can't get over how he acted the night of the fire." Her voice cracks a little and I look up to see if her face shows what I thought I heard in her voice, and it does. Her eyes are rimmed with tears waiting to spill, but she continues, "I just don't know what I'd do if something happened to Jack. I feel like he was so close to danger that night, and I would've expected Noah to be there, and he wasn't. I know Jack ended up being fine, but I just get swallowed by the what-ifs sometimes." She glances at Jenna with guilt written all over her face., "Shit, Jenna, I'm sorry, that was insensitive of me. I'm so sorry." She covers her face with her hands., I don't think Jenna can tell but I can see that those tears she was holding back spill over.

Jenna reaches for both of Kristen's hands and tells her what we've all spent months and years figuring out. "My grief is mine, but it doesn't negate anyone else's or their fears. That includes you. I know your fear all too well, but I won't ever hold it against you." She takes her napkin and wipes Kristen's cheeks. "Take it easy on Noah though, eh? He carries around a lot of guilt as it is. He doesn't need you to add on more."

Before Kristin has a chance to respond I see Sherri waltz in through the front door.

"Jenna, Sherri's in town! Did you know?"

She smacks her head with her hand. "Oh shit! Yes, I did, and was so excited to tell you when I got here but then we got side tracked." She laughs. "I guess that's not unusual but yeah, she's moved back. Finally! She's starting back at Liam's next week, but I'm sure she'll help over at Jack's this weekend too. She can help us figure out how to gather everyone we need to help."

Jenna and I both go to meet her when she's halfway to our table and wrap her in a big group hug.

"Hey lady, I'm so glad you're here!" I swat Jenna "Miss Jenna here didn't even tell me."

"I was getting to it." She kisses Sherri's cheek. "So happy to have you back, bestie. Come meet Jack's sister, Kristin."

We make our way back to the table and introduce them before we all sit again and fall into an easy chat, planning and organizing Operation Replant. Jenna makes a list of all the local business owners that we know will be more than willing to help out. I'm going to go see Cara down the street. Kathy at the bakery isn't a young woman anymore, but she'll send her sons and I'm sure she'll provide lots of baked goods to keep everyone motivated. I can make my rounds that I usually do for work, and we'll have a crowd by the time I'm done. Liam will be able to convince Paul and his brother Justin to come for at least one of the days and if every one of those people brings a couple friends, we can probably get this done this weekend.

Sherri's making a note in her phone of who she needs to go visit and sweet talk. She looks up and says, "Hey, can't Noah get a bunch of the guys from the department to help?"

Jenna scrunches up her face. "Oh, you probably don't know yet, but that's likely not going to work."

"I know he's not on the department anymore, but I'm sure the crew still care about him, and Jack, especially considering it's a *fire* we're rebuilding from. If they're off duty I'm sure they'd come if he asked. I'll talk to him, but I think that's a sure thing we can count on too!"

Jenna makes crazy eyes at me and then a side eye back to Sherri, who doesn't notice because she's typing out a text to Noah. Jenna stares at her, waiting for her to lift her gaze from her phone. When she finally does, she startles at the look on Jenna's face, I cover my laugh with a cough and keep my eyes planted down looking into my coffee.

Jenna implores her. "How do you know he's not on the department anymore? You just got back to town this morning!"

Sherri laughs nervously, but holds up her phone. "Fancy little thing called a telephone!"

"Ha-ha, you're so funny. But seriously, is there something going on with you and Noah? I know I asked you before, but you always shut down when I bring it up. I won't be mad, if that's what you think. I told you I just want you both to be happy!"

"There isn't anything going on, not really anyway. I don't know. We do talk a lot. He told me about everything before you did, the fire and Charlie, I mean. I just pretended I didn't know when you told me because I didn't want to have this conversation." She winces slightly. "And I knew he was going to quit the department before he did it. He's really struggled since Mark died. I know everyone has, so I don't mean anything by that, but I think he and I just found some common ground with our grief. It's not about that anymore; now I think we're just really great friends and I don't really know if there's more to it than that or if there ever could be. I know he's focusing on Jack and Charlie and getting the brewery up and running before Christmas, so he isn't really thinking about anything like that either. I just want to be here for him if he needs me, work here at Liam's, and just get back to living. I think that would feel really good right about now."

None of us have much of an argument for that. Kristen looks a little uncomfortable, maybe at witnessing such a deep conversation with someone she's just met and thankfully, Jenna drops it with a smile and another clink of our mugs. "Here's to that!"

CHAPTER
Twenty-One

Jack

Unfamiliar cars keep driving in and parking in front of my barn. I say unfamiliar, but I've seen them all before, whether around town or at my farm at Christmas time, but what are they doing here today? Every time I glance out the window another one is pulling in. Finally, I see Sara and Kristin arrive together in Sara's Jeep, with Jenna and Sherri not far behind and Noah, with Charlie riding shotgun, bringing up the rear. They've done something. They've planned this, for everyone to be here today to plant trees. I should be happy, grateful at least, but I can't help the knot in my stomach and the weight I feel on my chest. Guilt, shame, anger. I don't know if I can name it any of those, but it feels like shit. I can't help that it translates to being pissed off. They went behind my back and dragged the whole town into my mess. I've spent the last ten years doing favours for everyone in town to make up for the help I asked for to plant trees when I first took over.

I can't stomach this again.

I storm out onto the porch and let the wooden screen door slam hard behind me. Sara jumps at the noise and lifts her head to meet my icy glare, startling when she makes eye contact. I can tell by her expression that she was expecting this. She knew this would upset me and did it anyway? I know her, I know her heart was in the right place. I want to understand that she was just trying to help, but I can't get past how small this whole thing makes me feel. And she should have known *that.* As if it wasn't bad enough that I had to watch my crop burn, now I have to watch the whole town pity me for it and go out of their way to make my life easier.

No. I can't do it.

"Sara!" I yell across the yard, louder than I intended, because she jumps in surprise and moves quickly to join me on the porch. The nervous look on her face twists my gut, knowing I put it there, but another part of me is glad she's uncomfortable. She deserves to feel a little bit of what I am right now. I send a glare at my sister too before I spin on my heel and go back inside. I have no doubt she was also a mastermind in this.

Sara follows me into the kitchen. I can feel her nervous energy and I really do hate it, but I hate how I'm feeling inside even more. I don't turn around to look at her. I won't be able to handle seeing the hurt in her eyes, so I lean against my sink and keep my eyes looking out the window; front row seat to the whole fucking town out there gathering shovels and moving trees to the field.

"What the fuck are they all doing here?" I say between clenched teeth.

She stumbles over her words, "They... umm... they're here to help plant the trees. Why are you so angry? Jack? What's going on?"

I lean forward and cross my forearms on the counter in front me, resting my head on top. I have to get myself together. I want to scream in anger but at the same time I want to crumble to her every whim. How can I feel such conflicting emotions at the same time?

Mumbling into my arms hides some of the heat behind my words. "Why am I angry, Sara? How can you ask that? This isn't how I wanted to do this and you know it. If I needed their help I would've asked." I stand up straight again and am faced with that same view out the window. Seething feels safer than yelling at this point. "I don't know how you could've ever thought that I would want to be indebted to all these people, again!" My jaw is clenched so tight on that last word I think I may have chipped a tooth. I'm trying like hell not to raise my voice at her, but I don't know how to make her understand how much she has taken from me by doing this.

I can feel her coming up close behind me so I turn around to face her before she can touch me. I know if she touches me, I'll forget about any of this and just want to hold her in my arms. That won't solve anything though. Kristin wants me to talk about my feelings more, well here goes. "I know I sound like an asshole, hell, maybe I am an asshole, but I don't want their help. Not today and not tomorrow or next week!" I take a deep breath in and let it out, trying to calm my tone. Fuck, I hate this, but I manage my next words without emotion. "I had it handled."

I can tell that I've pissed her off now by the colour that stains her cheeks. "You had it handled?" Her volume rises on that last word. "Handled, Jack? Do you even see the mess you're in?! We couldn't have ever got those trees planted in time for them to get good growth and roots before they'd shrivel up and die. Saving your ego is going to be at the expense of what's left of your business. Are you shitting me right now?"

"No, I'm not shitting you! I needed to do this on my own. I thought you, of all people, would understand that! You've done your whole life by yourself. But I guess it's fine for you to push us all away and never give an inch but as soon as someone else wants to do the same you push your way through and do whatever the fuck you want!"

I know those words will hurt but I'm hurting too and sometimes hurt makes us do and say stupid things. I just don't understand how she can think this is any different than what she's done her whole damn life.

She shakes her head, and I can see tears welling on her lower lids. Fuck, if she cries, I'm done for.

Her voice is quieter now, calm almost. "Jack, you've taught me so much about being vulnerable, about asking for help and letting people in. You've shown me it's okay to be myself, that I don't have to keep walls up to stay safe. You keep me safe. You are all I need, nothing else matters anymore. I can quit my job, I can deal with my parents, and cry myself to sleep missing my sister. I can get frustrated arguing with Andi, but at the end of the day, you're there with your strong arms and your love. They keep me afloat and they make the rest of it matter so much less. I thought I did that for you. I thought you had let me in, but you didn't. You just wanted to break down my walls to collect a trophy or what? 'I got Sara Ryan to fall in love with me', what is the prize for that Jack?"

Her voice cracks and tears spill over her eyes and down her cheeks and I freeze. I want to reach for her, but I can't seem to make my limbs move. I don't know how to make this better. She's wrong. She couldn't be more wrong about that. I love her with everything that I am, and I have for so long. That has nothing to do with this. This is about me and being good enough for her. I don't know how to tell her that when she's already drawn these crazy conclusions. I just don't want all these people dragged here to clean up my mess. My silence doesn't help my case any because she turns to leave. I finally take a step towards her, grabbing her wrist before she makes it out of the kitchen.

"Sara." As I say her name, she yanks her hand out of my grip and turns around. The green in her eyes is sharp and fierce and I'm reminded again why I love her so much. She is strong and loving and in that she carries so much power. "Sara. Listen, it's not like that at all. You know I love you, more than anything. This is about me, about me earning your love in return, being good enough, holding it together well enough, being the one that has it all together so that I can hold you together too. I spent so many years getting to where we are, to where you could see me as exactly what you need. Please, let me be that."

Her eyes soften slightly at my words, but her tone is as sharp as ever. "I am not going to break, Jack! I'm allowed to be sad and maybe even have breakdowns once in a while, but I am not a fragile piece of crystal that you have to handle with care. You have to feel your own feelings and stop pretending to be protecting mine! This," she waves her hand between us, "will never work unless you get your head out of your own ass and treat me like an equal." She turns and quickly strides to the front door. Before she lets the door slam, she turns around and says, "I love you, but you are not my saviour. You make my life better, and you have brought so much love and joy back into it that I didn't think I would ever experience again, but I didn't need saving and I still don't. Neither do you, and that's not what this is. This is community, a group of people who love you and want to support you. You will not be indebted to them and how dare you suggest they'd expect that. If you don't know how to receive the love and care that you give to the rest of us, then I don't know what we're doing here. I quit my job yesterday because you've helped me to see how strong and capable I am. That isn't because I'm relying on you, it's because I can rely on myself! Let me do the same for you! I don't want to be in a one-sided relationship where I'm the only one who is ever in need. That's not love Jack, that's you having a hero complex."

The sound of the wood on the screen door smacking against the doorframe as she leaves is like a hammer striking my heart.

CHAPTER

Twenty-Two

Jack

I eventually get over myself and join the whole damn town that has congregated in my field and is busy planting trees. Sara doesn't give me a single glance the whole day, nor the day after. She packs up and leaves in her Jeep before I even know she's gone. I can't believe she quit her job. I'm so damn proud of her! I know this is the best choice for her and for Andi, but she needed to reach that place on her own. I want to celebrate with her but instead I'm here, trying to rebuild my life and feeling like I've lost the only part of it that truly mattered. The fire seemed so devastating at the time–don't get me wrong, it was, and still is–but this weekend has shown me how much more there is at stake. All the effort Sara put into gathering everyone paid off. Even more people showed up Sunday and we actually got all these damn trees in the ground. If I didn't see it with my own eyes, I wouldn't believe it. Three thousand trees planted in two days. This town really does come through for its own.

Like she's reading my thoughts Cara walks by and stops to rest her hand on my arm. "This is what it is to be a part of Balsam River; you know that, Jack," she says. "You don't owe anyone a thing."

Kathy follows her, carrying the last cardboard box heaping with chocolate chip cookies that she brought for everyone. She kisses my cheek as she presses the box into my hands and walks away without a word. Paul and Justin and a bunch of their friends that I just met today wave and holler their goodbyes as they get in their cars and drive home. So many people, young and old, some I've known my whole life and some I just met. I'm so grateful for all of them. I say thank you to everyone, wishing there were more words to express how I'm feeling. I wish Sara was here. I wish I could show her how grateful I am that she did all of this for me.

Noah and Liam hang around while Jenna and Sherri leave to take Charlie back to the Ryan's for evening chores with Brent. The tension between Sara and I all weekend isn't a secret, so of course, the first thing her brothers are wanting to know is what happened between us.

I don't know when these guys started acting like gossipy women, but I could really do without it right now. They are relentless, so I fill them in and wait for them to ream me out for being an asshole and treating their sister poorly. I deserve whatever it is they're going to throw at me.

I just can't wrap my head around my own bullshit and feelings, and that failure may have just cost me the most important thing in my life. The two most important things. Sara and Andi are everything. Without them, nothing else matters.

Noah chimes in first. "So, you're pissed at her for organizing this weekend? Your masculine pride has been questioned and she feels inadequate because you're always the rescuer. Sounds like you both need to shut the hell up and be there for each other, rather than doing whatever you think the other one wants or needs. That sum it up?"

"Fuck off, Noah." I run my hand through my hair in frustration. How does he make it sound so simple?

He takes a step back and smirks. "Hey, don't shoot the messenger. It's easy to tell it how I see it when I'm not the one involved. Mark and I had to spell it out for Liam last year too." He starts laughing now as Liam punches him in the arm. "Dumbass couldn't get out of his own way. Look at him now, so clearly I know a thing or two about love."

Liam shakes his head, but his tone is light when he says, "Sure you do, look at your track record. Long term relationships…zero, short term relationships…zero. You have girls lining up to marry you and you can't run away fast enough." He looks at me then. "Noah is only good at giving advice. He wouldn't survive one week with the emotions running through him that you're feeling right now. I know you're unsure right now, Jack, but you gotta make it right with her. You guys are the real deal. You must know that."

"I'm not unsure of Sara, I'm unsure of myself. She isn't wrong about anything she said, and I can't change who I am overnight. Shit, Kristin has been trying to get me to deal with this shit since we were kids and I thought she was crazy. Sara is showing me that I have baggage too, but I don't think she wants to carry it. I don't want to ask her to carry it. I've only ever wanted to lift her up, to make her happy. If I'm going to bring her down with me and make her feel like she's anything less than perfect then I have no idea how I'll live myself. I can't. I won't be that guy."

"Jack, you're missing her point completely. She told you that you're enough. She doesn't want the perfect version of you. That doesn't exist, I might add. She just wants you guys to work through this life together. I hear you; I'd do anything to make Jenna's life easier, but I can't if it undermines her own decisions. She's made that very fucking clear." He shakes his head and I hear his love for Jenna in his laughter. I know the two of them have been through it and made it out the other side. I just don't know what that looks like for me.

They drop the topic of Sara surprisingly easily and we move on to discuss the brewery. All the equipment arrived this week and a team is coming Monday to assemble everything. The first batch should be fermenting by the first week of September. I don't know much about it, but Noah's done his research. He says that takes two weeks. He's waiting on a bottler and all the supplies, and he wants to run a bunch of batches before opening to make sure the flavour is right and to build stock. His goal is to open to the public on December 1st. I can't believe how fast he's pulled this off but that's typical Noah. When he wants something, he wants it yesterday and not much stands in his way.

Jenna and Sherri come back to retrieve them, but before they pull away Noah calls to me from the backseat of Liam's truck. "Come over in a bit for a late dinner and have a couple beers with us! Around eight, sound good?"

"I don't know, guys; I'm exhausted and kinda feel like shit anyway."

"Come on. It'll help. Have a couple drinks, we'll BBQ and make sure it's not a late night. You need this, Jack. We'll see you at eight!"

Before I can protest again, they're gone. Liam's driving, asshole knew if he sped away I wouldn't be able to say no. I could just not show up, but the guilt is setting in already. They've done so much for me this weekend, and the last few weeks since the fire. The least I can do is have dinner and a beer with them. I retreat into my house to sulk by myself. It's so quiet with both Sara and Kristin gone. It turns out Jenna's house that she's been leasing is available and has been sitting empty, so Kristin moved into it this week. I don't really mind being alone, I've been alone for all of my adult life. But I'm not going to lie, I had really gotten used to the alternative.

CHAPTER

Twenty-Three

Sara

Noah: *Dinner and beer at my place, bring Andi, come over around 8:00.*

Sara: *I don't know, it's been a long ass weekend. I don't really feel like it.*

Noah: *Too bad, Sherri's here and Liam and Jenna are coming. Get your ass over here.*

Ugh, brothers suck. He knows how happy I am to have Sherri back in town, but why does he need to use it against me when I just want to snuggle on the couch with Andi. After she goes to bed I can crawl into my own and cry myself to sleep. I don't know what's going on with Jack. I couldn't face him all weekend. I did what I needed to do, helped with the trees because despite everything, my heart wants what is best for him and his business. I will always do whatever I can to help him, whether he wants it or not. I never considered that that's what would ruin us, but I won't compromise on this. I won't live my life stuffing my feelings and showing him a watered-down version of my love. He's not wrong that it took a long time to get to where we were, but that makes it all the more precious to me. I don't think that was an argument for his side, I feel that with everything that I am. I froze him out for seven years! How can he expect me to do anything but make up for that now?

I turn on the movie that Andi and I had planned to watch. She's still into all the Christmas movies. The Grinch is number one on her list so that's what we're watching tonight, neither of us caring that Christmas is months away. I give her a snack and tell her we're having a late dinner at Uncle Noah's. She's ecstatic, of course. She doesn't know her uncles suck.

A couple of hours later, I walk through Noah's front door without knocking. I make my way across his house to the back deck where I can smell them barbequing from my own house. I put my beer in the fridge and follow Andi out the sliding door. I stop in my tracks when I see Jack sitting at the patio table. He looks so tired and sad but also so damn good. His jaw is covered with the perfect amount of stubble; he never remembers to shave when he's busy. His eyes can't hide how exhausted he is but when he looks at me, they're so warm and full of love it almost melts my insides. His plaid button up fits him more than perfectly and I want to feel the cotton against my fingertips. My eye catches on his fingers wrapped around his beer bottle; they should be pressed against my skin. I want that back. I want everything I thought I would never have to live without again. I want to run into his arms and run back to my house to hide, all at the same time.

Noah's voice breaks my stare. "Okay you two, this ends here." I flash my eyes in his direction. What is he talking about? Why is Jack even here? I look around the deck and see that Liam and Jenna are snuggled on the outdoor couch with sheepish looks on their faces. Sherri isn't here yet, and maybe she's not even coming. Maybe this is an intervention for family only and Noah just used her name to get me here.

"Noah, what is going on? Whatever it is, this isn't the time." I glance towards Jack, where Andi has now inserted herself on his lap with her colouring book and crayons spread across the table in front of them. "The time or the place," I grit out between clenched teeth, nodding my head so he can see that asking Andi to be a part of this was not a good idea.

"No, little sister, this is the exact time and place." He points his finger at everyone, one at a time until he lands on Jack and Andi. "These people are your people. All of us." Then he looks at Jack and says, "And they're *your* people."

Andi looks up from her colouring and smiles her 'bright as sunshine' smile. "My people too, right, Uncle Noah?"

Noah grins like he's won the lottery, "Yes! Yours too! This is what you guys need to see, and I don't just mean Jack because he's a stubborn ass that won't ask for help. I mean you too, Sara." He comes toward me now and I can't decide if I should shut him down or shut up and listen. He doesn't give me a chance to decide anyway. He grabs my arm and tucks himself in so that he is now holding me by both arms while he stands behind me, clearly trying to prove a point by showing me '*my people*'. "I don't care if you don't ever let another person in, but for us, it's too late. You two are everything to each other and we've watched you dance around each other for too long to watch your pride ruin it."

"Noah, it's more than pride, and you know it. There is so much more going on here, issues we can't solve with a beer and a BBQ. Nor do I want to have this conversation with Jack, in front of my brothers, or Andi for that matter! What are you even thinking, setting this up? Have you lost your mind?"

Jack has yet to say a word, but I can tell that he agrees with me. He's letting Noah know where he stands by completely ignoring him and engrossing himself in whatever Andi's telling him.

Then Liam stands from where he's sitting, obviously these two have planned to tag team. I don't even want to hear what he has to say but I almost laugh out loud when I hear Jenna mumble, "Oh boy, here comes a 'Liam' speech."

He scowls at her but starts his speech anyway. "Sara, it's not that we think you'll hash out all of life's problems right here and now, we just want you to see what you have and what is important. It's this! Jack is here, Andi is here, and so are we. This is our family, and we are here for each other. You have been the caretaker for years now and we've let you. I don't know why we let you carry so much but we did. I think we thought we were helping you by letting you keep yourself busy. We were wrong. We have all learned in the worst ways possible how fragile life is and we aren't taking anything or anyone for granted. We all know this, but then something like this comes up and we stuff our feelings down and don't acknowledge the work that needs done to make these relationships work!" He turns to Jack and throws his hands in the air, clearly aggravated now. "Jack! You are not an island. You are not our life preserver either. We love you, man, so let us be there for you too. Talk to us about what it was like losing your mom, let us know how things are with your dad, share when you're worried about Kristen, tell us when you're behind on the farm and you need a hand. This isn't just about you and Sara. That part is a Jack problem, through and through. It affects us all, but it ends here."

Noah claps his hands together. "Okay guys, this is heavy, we know. What we actually planned was to give you both this little speech and then we're going to take our burgers and Andi back to your place. Now you'll have time to figure your shit out, without your *brothers.*" His imitation of me could use some work but he continues anyway. "We know this fire shook things up. We're all still raw from... everything... from life, but you have to know there's always life after death. Your world can feel like it's falling apart and like there's nothing left of it, but there will always be something new growing from the ashes. It won't be the same, or the one you planned but it's still a life, and it's still worth fighting for. There's hope in that, and if you can't see it yet, you aren't fighting hard enough."

They all exit at the same time, in a much too organized fashion, with

Jenna scooping up Andi on her way by. I hear them whispering inside, gathering food and beer, and then finally the front door closes. Two minutes later I hear my own front door open and close. Then all there is, is silence. It's just the two of us. To fight for the life we want.

While I'm deciding what I'm going to do next, standing like a dolt in the middle of the deck, Jack rises slowly from his chair and walks just as slowly towards me. He's acting like I'm a wild fawn that could bolt at any second. Oddly enough, he wouldn't be too far off. I've considered running from this spot exactly fourteen times in the twenty-ish minutes since I've been here. He's standing directly in front of me now. That smell that can only be Jack envelopes me and I want to swoon. Sometimes I hate that he has such a visceral effect on me. It wasn't always this way. But then he broke down my walls, while piecing my heart back together.

I extend my hand toward him and brush my fingers along the stubble on his jaw. The roughness against my soft fingertips sends a shiver down my spine.

I don't know where to start, so I start by telling him exactly what's in my heart. "Jack. You never had to earn my love or become good enough. You always were, I just wasn't paying attention. When I do things like this weekend to help you, I'm not trying to take anything from you. I'm just trying to give back a tiny bit of the love and care you've shown me. You've always been here for me, a constant presence, persistent and everlasting, always waiting. You're Jack. My Jack. You never stopped showing up and showing me what love looked like. It wasn't a test for you to pass, I just needed to catch up. I did. I'm here now. I need you to see me as someone who can love just as hard as you. You crashed through my walls so hard I didn't even realize that you had your own, but I see them now and I want in." I hold his face in both of my hands and search his eyes. I don't know exactly what I'm looking for but something like hope would be really great right about now. "Please, Jack. Let me in."

He reaches up and places his rough palms over top of my hands. He slides them down to my wrists and pulls my hands away from his face, pressing them together, palm to palm. He is still holding them by my wrists, between us. He kisses my fingertips, so gently that if I wasn't watching I might not have felt it, but then he lets go and wraps his arms around me. He mumbles into my hair, "I'm so sorry Sara, I'm sorry I didn't see any of this before and that I lashed out at you."

The feeling of having him holding me again can only be described as coming home. It feels like nothing else matters and we can face anything as long as he holds me like this. How can one man, doing such a simple thing, bring out so much emotion and peace?

I don't want to ever leave.

He goes to pull away and I know we have more to talk about, but I can't right now. I just want this for a little while longer. "Hold me longer. Please, Jack." I squeeze my arms tighter around his waist and I feel his lips land softly on top of my head.

He whispers, "Anything for you, Sara." I think I'm falling in love with him all over again.

We stand there holding each other for who knows how long before I finally lean back and tilt my head up to see his handsome face. He smiles down at me like I'm the only thing in the world that can make him smile like that, and I think... maybe I am.

His face turns serious as he rubs his thumb gently across my cheek. "I'm going to do better. I know you think I'm enough, but I want to be more. I want to spend my life proving to myself that I deserve you. I know there's going to be hardships, hopefully no more fires." He smirks, and I'm pretty sure it's too soon to joke about that, but I guess if anyone can it's him, "I know there will be other things. We're going to get angry and be sad and have breakdowns."

Oh, he better not be mocking me right now. He quickly adds, "I mean I will have breakdowns, not you. Don't you look at me like that."

We both laugh and it feels so damn good. He turns around and grabs a napkin off the table, pulls a pen out of his shirt pocket–men are so weird–and starts scribbling something on the napkin.

Sara,

Just another note to remind you that you are it for me. This is it, we made it.

Love,

Jack

I shake my head and smile, but I take his pen from his fingers. I turn to the table with it to add my own message to his napkin.

Thank you for waiting, Jack.

I tuck it into his shirt pocket and pat it with my hand. "Are you done? Can I talk now?"

He bursts out laughing, but shakes his head. "No, love, I will never be done. I'm all in and there will be no more walking away. We are in this together from now on. We will live better and love harder; we'll do everything we can to rise from the ashes. We'll breathe hope into this new version of us and give everything we have to this love between us."

I push myself up on my toes the little bit that's needed to reach his lips and kiss him like it's the first and last time all wrapped into one.

Against his lips, I whisper, "I love you, Jack Turner."

That damn dimple is out in full force when he says, "I've loved you longer."

CHAPTER Twenty-Four

Sara

Three months of being a stay-at-home aunt and wanna-be novelist and I don't think I've ever been so content. I love that I get to take Andi to school and pick her up, I can be at all her riding lessons now, and she's started ballet, because we finally have the time. She's really thriving at school and at home. My parents are still being their usual invasive selves, unfortunately even more so, I think because they are seeing Andi a normal amount now. When they were constantly helping me out with her it was excessive, but they loved it. I think it's important and necessary for me to hold my position of authority with her, and they have to remain in the 'grandparent' role. After raising us four wild children, it just comes naturally to them to step into the parental role with her, but somehow, I have to convince them of how much it's hurting me and in the long run Andi too. Somehow.

Noah almost has Balsam's Brewery ready to open to the public. I have no idea how he accomplished everything in such a short time, but the man was on a mission. They've bottled six batches and now have a constant flow of brewing thanks to their five employees, plus Noah and Jack. Jack won't be able to help at this time of year in the future but this year he's got a lot of free time on his hands. I'm grateful to this project for keeping him busy and focused on the future. I don't want him to have to worry about whether he's going to make it next year with his family's business.

Noah blames himself for the fire; he thinks he should've made sure that Charlie could come to him before a crisis rather than after, which is crazy considering he didn't even know he was having trouble with friends. And he thinks if he had ignored the kid and helped fight the fire, then maybe it wouldn't have been as bad. I don't think it would've made a difference, because he's only one man. Those kids would have done what they were going to do with or without Charlie. I don't know if I believe how innocent he was in the whole scenario anyway. Jack and Noah are convinced he's a great kid, but that just doesn't add up for me. I've asked Noah to take over Andi's riding lessons for now, until I can figure out how I feel about this kid working so closely with her. I know I can't protect her from everything, Lord knows she's already been exposed to enough heartache, but nothing says I can't try. He just seems like bad news to me.

"Hey Sara, come out here! The sign is up!" Noah hollers from outside the barn. I finish unpacking the last case of bottles I was shelving for them and rush out the doors. They've been waiting weeks for the signage, and it finally arrived this morning. Noah designed and had individual letters ordered from a local carpenter, stained a rich cherry wood colour to stand out against the old, grey barn board. He's been working all morning at nailing them up above the double doors. He says they should be large enough to read from the road. Balsam's Brewery is on the cusp of making Balsam Trees the ultimate destination in northern Ontario for the whole Christmas tree buying experience. It'll really drive tourism up in the summer too. The river is a bit of a draw to the area already, but a local brewery was one of the only things that Balsam River was lacking. I can't wait to see this design he's been raving about.

"Oh no! What did you do?" I exclaim as soon as I see it.

Jack is standing solemnly off to the side, and Noah and Liam are splitting a gut in the middle of the drive. No one answers me, so my next question is, "Who is Sam?"

This has Noah hooting louder. "It was... an accident." He's trying to catch his breath and wipe tears from his eyes at the same time. When he's finally calm enough to speak, he says, "But I kind of love it."

"Well, I don't!" Jack yells as he paces from one side of the driveway to the other in front of the barn. He runs his hands through his dark hair, his cheeks flushed. He is pissed. And these two think it's hilarious.

What side of the fence am I going to fall on?

It is kind of funny, but Jack is way too particular to leave it this way. He has a sense of humour but this whole business venture is so important to him that I don't know if he can loosen his hold enough to change the entire name of it, for a joke no less.

I look back up to the barn wall and try not to crack a smile because he's watching me now.

SAM'S BAL BREWERY

Large, beautiful cherry wood letters, perfectly custom made, but Noah accidentally nailed them on the barn in the wrong order. Then with black paint it looks like he added another 'S', probably just to freak Jack out even more. It reads:

SAM'S BAL^{S} BREWERY

"Sam's Balls? Are you serious right now? You think this is funny? You've named our brewery Sam's Balls! Take it down, right now!"

Noah starts howling again; Liam never stopped. These men run businesses and are contributing members to society, but at this moment in time they are thirteen-year-old boys. I walk over to Jack and take his hand. "Hey, hun. I know you're upset but it is kind of funny, and by the look of them, you aren't going to get him to take it down. He loves it." I smirk over at my dumbass brother. Jack shakes his head, but I can see his lips curving up slightly, telling me he does see the humour, but he's worried about business more. "What if it becomes part of the attraction? Balsam's Brewery was kind of a boring name, no offense, but Balsam Trees could've used some sprucing up. What if this is a little joke that makes all the difference to attract clientele? It's a name they'll never forget anyway." I wince as he scowls at me and then up at the sign.

Noah approaches, calmly now. "Sara's right! This is fucking awesome! I swear to you I was just lost in thought and did not do it on purpose, though I kinda wish I had because I think it's great." He turns serious and looks at Jack. "We're partners, though. If you really hate it, I'll take it down."

Jack rubs his face in frustration. "Ugh! I don't know! It's too cold out here. Let's get inside and get warm and I'll think about it."

We rush inside the barn to get warm by the fire and I marvel at how this old barn has been turned into a rustic Christmas haven with a bar in the back and tables spread throughout. Noah throws himself down into a chair closest to the fireplace, rubbing his hands together in front of the fire. "Hey man, my fingers almost got frostbite putting those up there. Please don't make me take them down."

Jack throws his coat over a chair and slaps Noah on the back of his head on his way over to me. He wraps me in his arms from behind. "You can be a real asshole, Noah. I don't know if you did it on purpose, but we'll make the best of it. Leave it if you want, but you're footing the bill to change everything else."

"Worth it," Noah says as he grins from ear to ear and high fives Liam.

I nuzzle myself back into Jack, as I smile and whisper, "You love him, and you know it."

A deep laugh rumbles against my neck. "Yeah, I do. Lord only knows why. Probably only because he led me to you."

The door flies open, snow and cold air coming with it as Andi runs in. "Auntie Sara! Auntie Sara! I'm going to be a flower girl!"

I laugh and rumple her hair. "We know, silly. Auntie Jenna and Uncle Liam have been planning the wedding for most of this year."

She rolls her eyes at me; she is only seven, right? Should that be starting already? She looks up at me like I'm clueless. "I knooooww! But they have a real day now. It's going to be on June 8th!"

I look to Jenna and then to Liam, who have trailed in behind her. They're both beaming. "Really? You guys picked a date?"

Jenna claps her hands with excitement. "Yes! We just had to confirm it all with Kathy and Cara today for catering, but it came up as an option because the photographer had a cancellation that weekend. It worked for everyone else, so it's done! We're going to do what you suggested; have it behind your house, on the riverbank. It's as close as we can get to having Amy and Mark there with us and their little sunshine here," she pats Andi's head gently, "is going to walk down the aisle in front of me with her favourite flowers."

I rush to her and throw my arms around her. "I'm so happy, Jenna. This is so wonderful!"

She wipes happy tears from her eyes and then squeezes my hands in hers. "Having you and Sherri stand up with me will mean so much to me. I can't wait to spend the rest of my life with your brother and being your sister-in-law."

Andi pushes her way between us and looks up at us both before she giggles and says, "Why do all my aunties and uncles marry each other?"

I laugh. "What do you mean? Aunts and uncles are usually married to each other."

She shakes her head hard. "No, I mean, mine are already my aunts and uncles and then they get married. I'm not getting any new uncles because Auntie Jenna is marrying Uncle Liam, and you are going to marry Uncle Jack." I gasp audibly at her assumption. She pauses but her hesitation isn't because of that. She rubs her chin like an old man thinking hard. "I guess he wasn't my real uncle and now he will be so that one doesn't count! And I get to call Kristin, Auntie Kristin after you get married, right? So, I'm getting an uncle and aunt out of it!" She claps her hands, yelling, "I can't wait." And then Andi runs to the back room where she keeps her toys, for when we're all here working together.

What just happened? I look around the room, quickly glancing at everyone, starting with Jack, then Noah, Liam and Jenna. All but Jack are hiding snickers and smiles. He looks like he wants to grin but is waiting to see my reaction. Ugh, this kid. I swear she will forever keep me on my toes. I choose to ignore this awkward moment because she's given me a lot to think about and I don't want to deal with it right now, so I clap my hands together and say, "Pfft, kids, eh?" Then I head back to the bar where I was unpacking bottles for the next batch of beer to finish.

Once I'm sequestered back behind the bar I can't help my wandering mind. If Andi, at age seven, is so sure that her Auntie Sara and Uncle Jack are going to get married then what are we really waiting for? I convinced myself that I needed to be careful and take things slow for her sake, but she's not wrong. Nothing is really changing. He is already her uncle in every sense of the word even though not biologically, and he means everything to her, like I know she does to him. I didn't choose to raise my sister's daughter, and I would give anything to have Amy here doing it herself, but if I could choose anyone in the world to be by my side while I do, it'd be Jack.

CHAPTER

Twenty-Five

Jack

What a week this has been. I feel like I've been completely run off my feet and all I want to do is curl up on Sara's couch with her on one side of me and Andi on the other and watch a cheesy Disney movie. Unfortunately for me that is not going to happen, since it's opening night for the brewery. Despite Noah's dumbass name change the place is packed and it's not just locals. He wasn't wrong that it attracted tons of people from neighbouring towns and even groups of people from further south than I'd expected. There isn't a whole lot to do in northern Ontario in the middle of winter, so I guess a new brewery with a stupid name is the top choice.

Sam's Bals Brewery. Noah is such an idiot. Who the fuck is Sam?

You don't want to know how many times I've heard that question today. It's a mystery and apparently, it's keeping people invested. Noah has the whole social media thing figured out, hashtags and some other tags and shit I know nothing about, but it must be working because the barn is full and everyone's happy to be here. I didn't think I'd love the crowd and atmosphere that came with running a bar... brewery, whatever. Not that I can take credit for running anything, but whatever part I do have in it is turning out to be really great. No one's pissed off with a beer in their hand, and at Christmas time to boot.

It was a great idea to open this time of year and truthfully it has really taken the sting out of not having tree sales this season. We've sold some smaller trees that I wouldn't have said were ready, but the odd person wanted them anyway. The girls have spent days making wreaths and pots and door swags to sell, using branches from the pines that I'll end up having double, from replacing with mature ones after the fire. Sara and Jenna's creativity is unmatched, and Kristin has settled back into town perfectly and keeps up with Sara and Jenna like she's been a part of their crew all along. Sherri's been spending lots of time here helping Noah get ready for this opening too. It's truly amazing how much they've done for us all. I'm not being an ass about it, I'm grateful, and leaving it at that.

"I can't believe how successful your first day was!" Sara exclaims as we all gather in the barn with take-out breakfasts, ready to clean up and prepare for today's crowd. Will I ever stop calling it the barn? Probably not.

Noah scowls across the room at her. "Ye have little faith, sister. I knew it would be huge! Last night was everything I had dreamed, and more! I can't wait to see how this whole season turns out. I have so many ideas to draw crowds in the warmer months. It's going to be awesome."

His face lights up when he talks about anything to do with the brewery, and not just when he's talking about Sam's balls, though that seems to get him the most excited. It's really anything to do with the business. He just gets so animated and excited. It really made me realize how unsettled he was before. I think we chalked it up to grief, I know I did anyway, but it was more than that. It was definitely discontent, and he's looking so much better now that he has this passion project to focus on.

Andi tugs on my arm. "Uncle Jack, can I go outside to play? I'm all done eating."

"Sure, peanut, just stay close to the barn. You know the rules." I run my fingers down one of her long blonde braids and marvel at her beauty. I stare at her in amazement almost as often as I do Sara. How did I get so lucky to have these two beautiful ladies in my life? I would never wish to be put in this position of looking after and raising Andi instead of Mark, but fuck it's hard not to smile when I look at her beautiful green eyes. They're enough like Sara's that they're familiar, but truly identical to how Amy's were. I don't know what her future holds, but I can guarantee I will be a part of it. I don't know what the awkwardness was last week with Sara, when Andi mentioned us getting married, but after this weekend is out of the way I am going to get to the bottom of it. If she's doubting for a second that we're headed in that direction, I'm going to lose my shit. I know she didn't believe in forever before, but I thought I'd broken down all those walls, I don't care if I have to start all over, she will be mine and forever is all I'm settling for. Andi deserves more than forever after what she's been through, and I will give her everything I've got.

"Uncle Jack! Uncle Jack!" Her little voice screaming brings my heart to my throat for a second, but then I hear the joy behind the shriek and relax. I look around and see that everyone else is still immersed in their food or conversation, except for Sara. She makes her way over to me and takes my hand, leading me to the door where Andi is bouncing up and down on her toes.

"Come chalk with me! Please!" She drags out her please like there's a chance in hell I would ever say no.

Sara says, "Can we draw pictures on the side of the barn? It'll wash off."

I think about it for a second and she's right. Shit, I don't even think I'll want to wash it off. If people like the place being called Sam's Bals Brewery, surely they won't be offended by some chalk drawings done by our family.

Sara continues, "There really isn't anywhere else to chalk around here because everything is gravel or snow-covered right now."

I smile and grab Andi's braided pigtails. "Of course you can decorate my barn. The most sought-after artist in Balsam River is here on my farm! I can't wait to see what she creates!"

She grabs my hand that isn't holding Sara's and drags us both around the side of the barn. She has a whole bucket of various colours of chalk and gets to work. I set myself up down the wall a little and draw her a horse in front of barn doors that look like Brent's. I draw a sun and blue sky above it, and that's the extent of my skills. Her and Sara are giggling at something they've done, and I look up to see what's so funny. They both catch my eye and turn into each other, laughing harder now. I shake my head. These two, sometimes I forget who's the kid and who's the adult, but I love how soft and free Sara is when she's with Andi. That little girl is the only person in the world that can truly soften Sara down to her core. I hope she knows how lucky she is to have her.

I make my way over to them and they run about ten feet back from the barn and spin back around to face me. The looks on both of their faces are the most peculiar I've ever seen; Andi is beaming but also looks suspicious. Sara is definitely happy, but she looks a little melancholy, reminding me that sadness still lingers in her all the time, and likely always will. I wonder if that will ever not break my heart.

Andi yells, "Turn around, Uncle Jack!"

I turn to look at whatever masterpiece they've created on the side of my barn and when I see it; it takes my breath away. They've drawn three stick figures standing amongst rows of Christmas trees. There's a little person with long blonde hair standing beside a taller one with long hair and on the other side of the little girl, is a taller than humanly possible man with dark hair and whiskers on his face. I bark a laugh as my roaming eyes make it to that detail. I really need to start shaving more often. The woman is in a white dress with a veil on her head and above the man's head, Andi has tried to write as neat as a seven-year-old can, My Real Uncle Jack. Written neatly below all three of the people it says:

This is it, we made it.

I spin around to look at where they're standing, because I need to see Sara's face. I need to get a read on her and see if I can determine what all this means. I don't want to hope that her giggles mean that she no longer feels any awkwardness about Andi bringing this stuff up, but did she help her? Did she draw this? She definitely wrote that message at the bottom. We made it.

I need to see her and touch her and make sure that this is all real. Before I can even take a step towards her, she's right there in front of me, smiling softly and looking up into my eyes. Andi follows and comes to stand just a little between us. She looks up at her aunt and then back to me with a grin that would put the sunshine to shame. "Uncle Jack, will you be my real uncle? Auntie Sara wants to marry you!"

My eyes snap to Sara's. What the fuck is going on? This is crazy. My mind is reeling, thinking of how I can safely walk backwards out of this conversation to keep Andi from taking this any further. The last thing I need is her spooking Sara when I haven't had a chance to make my intentions clear to her again. But when I meet Sara's eyes, I don't see panic. I don't see fear or anxiety or anything that even remotely resembles being upset in any way. She's still smiling, and her smile is one of the most genuine I've ever seen from her. She takes my hand and holds Andi's in her other one before she takes my breath away all over again. "Jack, you have loved me longer, but you will never love us more than we love you. You are everything we never thought we would get in this life. You love us both unconditionally, you show up and never leave, and you've given us both a reason to believe in forever again. I think you've waited long enough." She drops her eyes down to Andi and then back up to me. With a confidence that I have never heard in her voice, she says, "Will you marry me? Be Andi's 'real uncle' and be my husband."

All I can do is stare at her. My throat feels like it's burning with the pressure to stop tears from spilling from my eyes. Do men get proposed to? Do they cry when they do? Well, they do now. Screw Noah thinking

I have any masculine pride bullshit.

This beautiful, smart, creative, out of this world shocking woman is handing me everything I've ever wanted.

I grab them both around their waists and haul them up against my body. Andi scrambles with her legs and arms and climbs me like a monkey and I hold Sara tightly, lifting her feet off the ground as I spin them both around. Their squeals are the sound of pure joy and I will never get enough of it.

I set them both down and kneel in front of Andi. I place a kiss on her forehead and take both of her hands and place them on my chest over my heart. "Andria Davis, I solemnly swear to be the best real uncle that I can be. I promise to always take care of you and your Auntie Sara and to always be there when you need me. I will make sure your Daddy would be proud that I have been given this job of taking care of you, and I will always make all my decisions based on what I think your Mommy would do." I lift both of her hands and kiss her palms. "Now, walk slowly, but you can go and tell Uncle Noah and Uncle Liam that you have another real uncle."

She wraps her arms around my neck and squeezes with all her might. She whispers into my ear, "I love you, Uncle Jack, thank you for loving us so much." Before I can respond, she lets go and is running around the back of the barn. So much for walking slowly to give me time here, but at least that's the long way to the front door.

As soon as she's out of sight I turn back to Sara, I'm not gentle when I grab her and crush her up against my chest. I don't think it needs to be said, but just in case, while my face is buried in her hair at the crook of her neck, I softly tell her, "Of course I will marry you."

I pull back and raise my head so I can see the look on her face and her eyes are brimming with tears, happy tears for once. I kiss her forehead just like I did Andi, and I watch her close her eyes as she smiles through her tears. I dip my head to press my lips to hers. It ends too soon, but I want to kiss away every tear that she ever sheds. My lips gently brush each cheek where tears are slowly streaming down and then I use my thumbs to dry them completely. "No more tears, love. Don't cry for me or for us. For as long as forever is, you will be mine and I will kiss and dry every tear that falls."

Her fingers tangle in my hair as I move my kisses down to her collar bone. I can feel her body tense against me, and the goosebumps rise on her skin. The sun is shining but it's still cold as hell out here, yet I know those chills are for me. She is my everything and I am hers.

She presses her head down to meet me where I'm gently kissing her skin and whispers into my ear, "I love you, Jack."

I lift my head and kiss her lips one more time. Her breath hitches as she lets me in and I let her know just how much she means to me. The taste of caramel and coffee takes over all my senses and I think I will never get enough of her.

As tradition would have it, Noah comes barreling around the side of the barn yelling, "What's Andi talking about?"

I break our kiss with a laugh, but I lightly feather my lips to the side of her head taking in the scent of her lavender shampoo and whisper into her hair, "I've loved you longer."

Sara rolls her eyes but smiles at her brother and answers him with a cheeky tone. "She's talking about us getting married. Because we are. Happily ever afters are real and all that crap."

She smiles and then giggles when I swat her ass and remind her, "Hey, it's not crap. This is it, Sara, we made it."

She laughs loudly and kisses me again while Noah hoots and hollers to the others.

CHAPTER

Twenty-Six

Sara

If walking on a cloud was a real thing, then that's what I would have been doing these last three weeks. Christmas went by in a whirlwind; it was a whole new experience, feeling so many conflicting emotions at the same time. After losing Amy, there was no conflict, it was just sadness, I found zero joy for a very long time. This is so different. The wonder of Christmas with a child in the house was enlightening and amazing, but the sadness of it being our first Christmas without Mark stained so much of it. To see Andi slouch into a sadness that I couldn't bring her out of was the hardest part of it all. I was surprised how much caring and worrying for her trumped my own grief. With the one-year anniversary of his death being this week I thought this whole holiday season would send me into a spiral, but it didn't. I needed to stay afloat for Andi and with Jack's help, I think I did it. We supported her through her sadness without trying to take it away, we allowed her to feel it and then to feel joy when she was ready to, and it was so awesome to be with her when she had those moments. She made special homemade gifts for everyone and seeing her sharing them with family and the smile on her face when everyone lit up at what she'd made them was priceless.

I know Amy and Mark are with us in spirit and that they're so proud of the little girl that they created. I see more of Amy in her every day and it's a gift I never knew I needed. The guilt that I feel when I'm happy raising her, or happy planning my wedding with Jenna and Kristin, or happy doing anything is becoming less and less overwhelming. I am learning to allow myself the happiness that Mark spent years teaching himself he was allowed to feel. I am beyond grateful for the time we had with him before he was taken from us and that he used that time to show us all how to grieve better. I didn't think that was something that could be taught but he lived his life as an amazing example to us all and I want to be that person for others. Mainly for Andi but Jack too, and our children in the future.

New Year's Day snuck up on us all. Almost everyone is here, and we're gathering at our house for a family lunch to acknowledge the one-year anniversary of losing Mark. Andi is a little withdrawn today so I'm happy we planned this to be here instead of anywhere else. She will be able to retreat to her bedroom and be alone if she needs to be. Jack and I are keeping a close eye on her, and Jenna mentioned she is too. Of course that reminded me to be aware of how Jenna's feeling about all of this. It's so hard to remember everyone's feelings on days like this. I was so focused on Andi that I forgot about how the others are experiencing something like the trauma of that day all over again. Each of us have dealt and coped differently all year and it shows up the most on days like today. It's hard to know what to do for each other, but I'm glad we discussed it after Christmas and decided this gathering would be good for everyone and then everyone can do their own personal thing afterwards if they need more.

There's a knock at my door and I'm happy to see Kristin on the other side when I open it. I asked her to come but wasn't sure if she'd feel comfortable. She's as much a part of this family as Jack is now, but I know she doesn't always feel that way. She hasn't been back in town for long and her and Noah seem to have really butt heads and not been able to come back from it. It's important for her to be here for Jack, and I won't turn away anyone that has love to pour over my niece.

A low growl comes from behind me as I close the door and give her a quick hug. "What the fuck is she doing here?"

I spin around and hiss, "Noah! Watch your mouth with Andi around. And what's wrong with you anyway? She's a part of this family and I asked her to be here. You're being ridiculous."

Kristin pats my arm and leans towards me. "It's okay, Sara. He doesn't scare me."

Noah scowls. "I don't get why you want to be here. We're remembering and celebrating the life of a great guy that you didn't even know."

She rolls her eyes. "Oh, give me a break. I knew Mark when I was a kid and I love Andi and want to be here for her today. Not to mention Sara and my *brother!*"

"Don't stand there and act like you care about Sara and Jack. You're the reason they almost split up back in the summer!"

"Noah, that's enough. What are you talking about? She had nothing to do with Jack and I needing to figure our shit out and besides that, we're fine now. Better than fine. Why are you dredging up the past?"

He glares at me and the hurt in his eyes makes me take a step back. I hear it in his voice too, but maybe only because I know him so well. "Dredging up the past is her favourite pastime. She never lets me forget that I wasn't there for her brother when he needed me, right, *Kris?*"

"It's Kristin, and yeah, you're a shit friend, selfish cowboy, wannabe hero, and your ego is showing if you're threatened by my presence today. Get over yourself."

Noah scoffs, his hurt quickly replaced by anger. "Don't you think we've all been through enough? Why would you think it'd be a good idea to add more trauma and drama for Jack and Sara by setting up the whole town planting trees for him? You knew he wouldn't like it and you threw Sara under the bus to get your way without getting flack from your brother! You almost single handedly tore them apart. You say you love them and care for them and have the nerve to call me a selfish prick? Look in the mirror, *Kristin*."

She looks dejected for a moment, but it fades as soon as it comes. "I didn't expect Jack to be that upset and I definitely didn't know he would lash out at Sara. Don't you ever question my love or loyalty to my brother again. He and Sara both know I'm sorry for my role in their disagreement. And for your information, I like what I see when I look in the mirror. Can you say the same?" She's gritting her teeth to keep her voice low but with a confidence I can only dream of, she strides past him and heads straight to the living room where I hear Andi exclaim, "Aunt Kristin! You came!"

Noah steps closer to me and growls again. Why he feels the need to keep doing that I'll never know.

"Why would you ask her to come today and why is Andi calling her 'aunt'?"

I try to soften my voice even though he is driving me crazy and making me want to wring his neck. It's clear he's going through something because this is so far removed from happy-go-lucky Noah that I don't even know what to do with it. Liam showed us all what a grumbly asshole he could be when Jenna came back to town last year, but I've never seen Noah like this.

"Noah, what is this really about? She's Jack's sister. Andi can call her Aunt Kristin if she wants to, but more than that, she's not going anywhere. You can't keep going at her like this. Can you just try to be nice to her?"

"Me? Why are you telling me this? She's been a 'grade A' bitch to me since the day of the fire and it hasn't let up for a second. I don't see you over there telling her to be nice."

"What are you, twelve? Jeez, Noah!" I throw my hands in the air and walk past him to join the rest of the family. This is not something I have the capacity to deal with today. He will have to wait to get my full attention when I'm less overwhelmed by emotions and parental responsibility.

Sherri walks through the door a little while later and calls hello to us all in the other room. Noah rises from the couch, where he found a seat far away from Kristin, to greet her just as she rounds the corner into the living room. He shocks us all by wrapping her in his arms and placing a gentle kiss on her lips. My eyes widen in shock, Jenna has an 'I told you so' smile on her face, Liam is shaking his head with an uneasy smirk–clearly unsure of how this will go–and finally my gaze falls to Kristin. Her eyes are shooting daggers into the back of Noah's head. Just as quickly as he took her into his arms, he releases her and turns to face the room while taking her hand in his. Sherri's cheeks are bright red. She obviously did not plan to 'out' their relationship today, but Noah didn't give her much choice.

He sternly says to everyone, "We're trying this out, I don't want to hear shit from any of you. It's not your business, it's ours. Opinions are not welcome." Without making eye contact with any of us he leads Sherri out of the room and heads towards the kitchen.

"Well that's super weird," Kristin snarls. I can't hide my surprise at her tone. I'm sure it's written all over my face, but Jack shakes his head, silently telling me to ignore her.

He addresses her though. "It's been a while coming. I'm not surprised, they've gotten close since losing Mark. Their losses are different, but they've obviously found common ground so I'm happy for them. If they're happy and find support in each other, what more can you want?"

Replacing whatever heat I heard in her voice a moment ago with calm indifference, she replies, "I don't know, just seems like an odd match." She busies herself flipping through a magazine that's sitting on my coffee table, ignoring the rest of the conversation as we all share our opinions on this new development. I wish she and Noah could just get along. They're both going to be at Jenna and Liam's wedding and they'll both be a part of the bridal party for ours. Maybe if they get some space from each other between now and June they'll be in better spirits to deal with this animosity. Thankfully Noah will be distracted by Sherri, so that should help.

He's crazy if he thinks we won't all have an opinion on this. We're siblings and we aren't what I think of as normal, either. We're stupidly close and annoyingly involved in each other's daily lives. My parents are playing out back in the snow with Andi, so they missed the show, but they definitely will have an opinion too. They always do. Not that I think our opinions matter; I wholeheartedly agree that they need to figure it out themselves, but good luck trying to stop us from having them.

CHAPTER

Twenty-Seven

Jack

Business is booming and life is freaking good. Spring is trying to arrive in Balsam River but it's still pretty cold most days. Today happens to be the exception, so I'm getting a decent start on pruning the trees. Andi is working with me today, or walking with me while I work, but she makes a usually boring job much more interesting. She talks nonstop and asks a million questions, and it's my favourite job to be the guy that gets to answer them all. Did I mention Google is my friend?

The last few months have been mundane but in the best way possible. Sara and I have fallen into a routine of spending most weeknights at her house and when Andi is at the main house having a sleepover on weekends we spend the nights at my house. I don't know why she loves it so much but any chance we can she insists on being here. We've never had Andi sleep over here. We're not sure how she'd adjust to that or if there's any point to it anyway. She's happy in her home and I don't want to change that. We've been avoiding talk of how we're going to address the living situation with a permanent solution; not because we don't want a solution, but mostly because we don't have one. I can't leave the farm. The only reason staying at her place has been working is because of the time of year, but even now it drives me crazy when I have to leave them in the morning. Knowing they're going to be at home hanging out and I'm going to be working around the farm at my house; it's so simple but I'd give anything to know that they're both tucked in warm by my fireplace while I'm working on the farm. It doesn't feel like that's a viable answer because neither of us want to uproot Andi when she's been doing so well. So for now, we carry on and ignore the lingering questions.

Andi stops suddenly, mid-sentence and says, "Can I have my birthday party here?"

I laugh and tug her braid. "Your birthday isn't until the end of the month, silly girl. Don't you want to have it at your house like last year?"

She looks around like she's contemplating major life decisions. She stares back at my house for a long while then almost knocks me over with what she says next. "Why don't me and Auntie Sara live here?"

I choke on air and then stammer out a bunch of sounds that don't even resemble words. I look around hoping that Sara appears out of thin air to deal with this one. What the heck am I supposed to say? I don't know how to handle this stuff with her. What if I say the wrong thing?

Through the haze of my internal fears taking over, Andi giggles. "Don't freak out, Uncle Jack. I just wondered. You're getting married, so we're going to live together. You can't leave the farm because it's your work and Auntie Sara can work anywhere if she brings her notebook and computer. I just assumed we would live here and wondered why we don't already."

"How old are you turning this year? Fifteen?"

She bends over laughing hard, "No! I'm turning eight, you know that."

I smile and shake my head, running my hand through my too long hair. "I do know that; you just surprise me every day with how freaking smart you are."

"So, when are we moving here? Can we before my birthday? We could have my party in the barn! I love all the twinkling lights in there, it's so pretty."

My hair is going to need a proper combing after I'm done with this conversation. I'm sure I'm making a heck of a mess of it.

"You know, peanut, I don't really know what the plan is for that. Why don't we go explain your logic to Auntie Sara and see what she thinks."

I can't believe this kid. She is incredible. If she's this excited to move out here, there's no other reason for Sara to hold off. I know this is just the reassurance she needs to make the decision and then to make the move. It's so close, I won't let this chance slip through my fingers. If I have any say, I'm going to have my girls under my roof before the end of the month.

"Jack! You can't move all of our stuff in two days! There's no rush, we have time. The house isn't going anywhere. You're being crazy!"

"I am crazy. For you." I kiss her on the top of her nose gently and she swats me away, laughing.

After our conversation with Andi earlier today, Sara agreed to move in. She was as shocked as I was that Andi was so in tune with the situation and also okay with leaving the home that was once hers and her dads. We brought that up, not wanting to put ideas in her head but also not wanting her to ignore feelings she may be keeping to herself. We also didn't want to risk that she hadn't thought of that yet and would struggle with it after the move. She amazed us over and over again with her emotional maturity by saying that she will always love that house because it's where she lived with her dad, but that it was a different time now, with us, so we could live somewhere else and make new memories. We reminded her that 'her house' would always be on her grandparent's farm so she could go back there anytime she wanted. She, of course, had already thought of that so after that we told her she was right, and they could move in here as soon as they wanted to. Sara didn't quite believe me when I said that it was possible to do it this weekend. Andi was game, so two against one, we won.

"I texted Liam and Noah. Liam's on his way and Noah's at home so he's going to start loading his truck right away."

She shrieks. "What? He can't just go into my house and start packing my stuff! He won't even know what I want to bring, *I* don't even know what I want to bring! We might as well leave the house furnished for anyone that comes to visit, so they can stay there. We don't need more furniture here."

"Really? You don't want your own stuff? I just assumed. I'm sorry, hun. I'll text him back to hold up until we get over there. You were so obsessed with having your things when you moved from your apartment, rightfully so, but what's changed?"

She shrugs her shoulders and leans into me. "I don't know, your home feels like my home. It's not about the stuff, it's about you and Andi. If we're all here together I don't really care what the couch looks like. I was so lost before. I felt like those physical things were all that was keeping grounded in my identity, but when you ask what's changed, all I can say is everything."

This woman. She never ceases to amaze me. I can't wait to bring her home, to make her my wife, and I can't wait to do life by her side.

"Hey, Uncle Jack, what is this poking out of the ground?" Andi calls from the other side of the row I'm working on. I peer around the trees and see her kneeling in the dirt at the flower bed my mother planted the day before she died. My heart clenches, thinking of how I had stuffed those memories down for so long. Why did I try to forget her? I walk over to where Andi is gently fingering green sprouts pushing up through the soil.

"Those are irises. They'll be beautiful purple flowers in the summertime."

Her eyes widened in wonder. "Really? How did they get here?"

I smile, happy to finally be able to share my mother with someone else who's important to me. I kneel down beside her and rub some of the dirt between my fingers and thumb. "My mom and I planted them when I was even younger than you are now."

She snaps her head towards me in shock. "Your mom? Where is your mom? I've never met her!"

"My mom died when I was only five. She had an aneurysm in her brain." She frowns and I know her next question is going to be, what's that? "That's where a blood vessel is weak and it bursts, allowing blood to go places where it shouldn't. She wasn't sick before that, so we didn't know she had anything wrong and didn't get a chance to say goodbye. I remember being really sad and missing her at first, but I didn't really remember anything else about her for a really long time."

"You only missed her at first? That's weird. You don't miss her anymore?"

I chuckle. "It is weird, isn't it? I do miss her, but in a different way. I didn't remember her, so I didn't know what I was missing. It didn't feel the same as some other ways of missing people. I remember more about her now, like these flowers." I point to the little sprouts. "I didn't remember planting these until the night of the fire, but when I was running by here that night, I remembered. It sort of felt like it was my mom being here with me when I was struggling and needed her."

She frowns then sits down on her bottom and stares at her hands in her lap. "Sometimes I feel like I'm not a nice person because I don't miss Mommy the same way I miss Daddy."

My chest pinches tightly at the thought that this sweet little girl would think that there's anything about her that's 'not nice'. Emotions are hard enough for us adults to sort out, I can't fathom how this child is processing all that there is to feel when we lose loved ones, especially parents.

I sit down beside her and gently lift her into my lap so I can wrap my arms around her. "Andi, you are the sweetest and kindest almost eight-year-old I know. The reason missing them is different is because you didn't get to know your mom. I didn't remember mine for a long time, so there are memories inside me somewhere, but you never got to meet her or experience her love. You didn't get as many years with your dad as you deserved, but you had enough to know and to remember what you're missing, and that hurts. It might even hurt more and that's okay. Your mom and dad understand all this stuff and are watching over you and guiding you through your life and they always will, even when you're all grown."

She smiles up at me, a sad little smile that I hate seeing on her face. There's a slight dampness in her eyes, but hope in her voice when she asks, "You think so?"

"I know so. These flowers remind me that there is always hope. They bloom every year no matter what and now they will always help me remember that my mom is looking out for me even if she can't physically be here. If you want, we can share them; you can use them to remember the same things, and in the summer when they're big and tall and beautiful you can cut some and bring them into your bedroom to remind you."

She beams that 'bright as sunshine' smile at me again and jumps up. "I would love that. Thank you!"

Sara's voice startles me when she comes through the trees a few feet away from where I'm still sitting on the ground. "What would she love? You're not promising any more treats are you, Jack?"

Andi laughs loudly and tells her aunt all about the flowers and our moms and Mark, and how they're looking out for us even when we don't always know it. She bounds away through the rows of trees, in search of her next adventure, I'm sure. Sara steps toward me as I stand and wraps her arms around my waist. She reaches up as I dip my head and we meet in the middle for a kiss that's more sweet than passionate but it's still perfect. It's everything. She is everything.

"Thank you for being her person, Jack. She needs you as much as I do, maybe more. I'm so happy we can build this life for her, together."

"Me too, Sara, me too." I rest my hand on the back of her head as she lays it against my chest. I marvel at how soft the strands of her hair feel between my fingers. I will never take these two girls for granted. I will never take any of this for granted again.

I squeeze her tighter and whisper against the top of her head, "We never wish for tragedy, and we try to avoid it at all costs, but sometimes beauty can come from the ashes that are left behind."

Acknowledgements

Writing the acknowledgements for my second novel is even crazier than it was to write them for my first. I think every book I write will feel like it's for my sister. Written for her and because of her. She died suddenly in 2022 at the age of 37, and nothing has ever been the same, nor will it ever be again. It breaks my heart that she's missing this, but I believe she's here with us and isn't really missing a thing. So, it's just me, missing her.

I want to thank the entire Instagram (Bookstagram) community, it truly is a wonderful place to be. My Street Team, ARC readers and fellow indie authors. A special thanks to the ladies of Literary Poutine Posse, an amazing group of Canadian women lifting each other up on this crazy journey we're all on together. I would be lost without you.

Thank you to my wonderful editor, Sarah Ward. Your insight, and professionalism is indispensable to me.

Thank you, Ivan Semonchuk-MIBLART for the beautiful cover design, I couldn't be happier with how it turned out.

My cheerleaders: Savanah, you are my whenever, wherever. Thank you for listening to every scene as it played out, and for reading and re-reading and then listening some more.

Aly, you've believed in me since before I knew there was anything to believe in. This grief is heavy, but you carry some of it for me and I am so grateful.

Heather, thank you for reading contemporary just because you love me! Your ideas, input and opinions mean the world to me!

Laura, your cheerleading and love is what kept me going on the days I didn't know if I would ever finish. When the words don't come out right, you're there to make sense of them.

The love and support from my family and community has blown me away, but I am especially grateful to my parents. I know they didn't understand my need to read and write all day long as a child, but they never diminished my love of the written word and now I'm an author, just like I said I would be one day! I am so grateful to be alive in a time when indie publishing is a thing. Thank you for everything you've done that led me to this.

Jordon, thank you for being my very own love story. You make everything easier.

Aaron, Melanie and Eden, you inspire me and support me, and you've loved me through it all. I will never be able to show you how much I love you. You are everything.

You have all helped make this book into the amazing, finished product that it is. I appreciate you so much.

Last, but certainly not least I want to thank my readers. You took a chance on me reading my debut novel, One Life to Live, or you've just found me in From the Ashes. Either way you put your time and heart into reading my story and I am so grateful to you.

It is such a blessing and a privilege to be able to share these stories and characters with you. I hope you love them as much as I do.

Blessings,

Athena

About the Author

Athena is a homeschooling mom and wife from Ontario, Canada.

Being the youngest of eight, in a close-knit farming family was the best way to grow up. She thinks this is why she values the love of family and friends above everything else.

She lives with her high school sweetheart turned husband and three kids on his family's horse farm and couldn't have dreamed up a better place to raise her family.

She can be found on their back deck reading or writing with coffee in hand any time of day...as long as it's after 9am.

Growing up with her only sister as her best friend in a house with six brothers created an unbreakable bond that she draws on daily. Despite her sister's untimely death their connection lives on, even in her absence, she was the inspiration behind so many things. Losing her brought a new perspective to life.

No regrets. Take the trip, buy the cottage, eat the ice cream, and write the book (or books).

Printed in Great Britain
by Amazon

42201819R00116